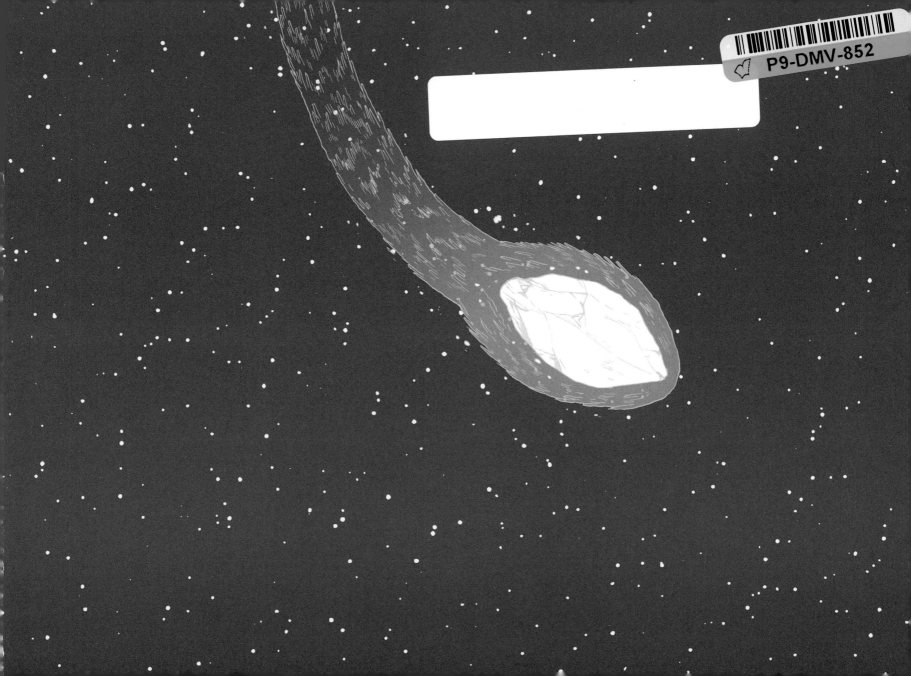
P9-DMV-852

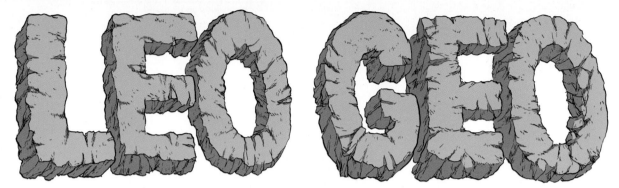

LEO GEO

AND THE COSMIC CRISIS

BY JON CHAD

NEW YORK

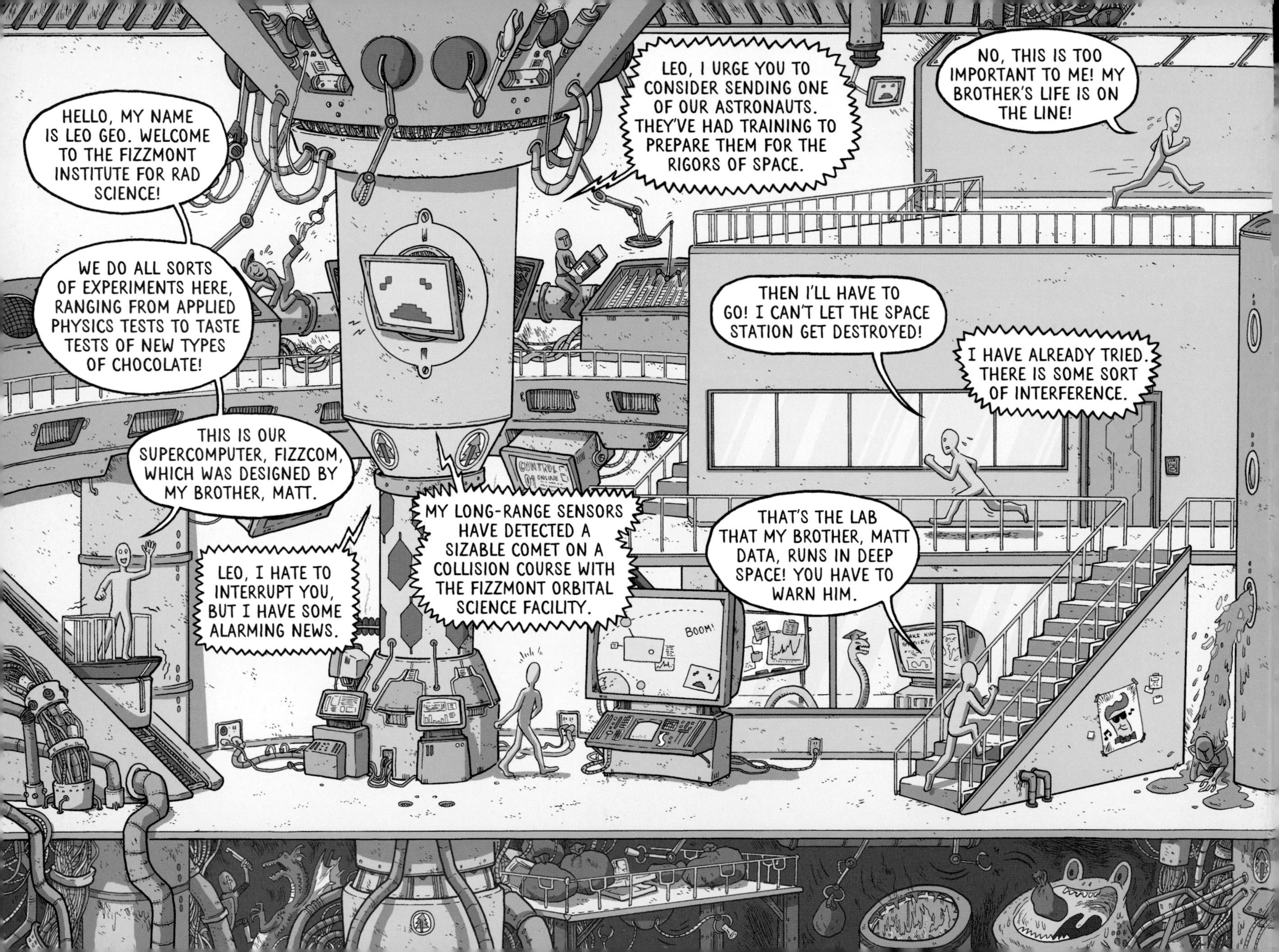
HELLO, MY NAME IS LEO GEO. WELCOME TO THE FIZZMONT INSTITUTE FOR RAD SCIENCE!
WE DO ALL SORTS OF EXPERIMENTS HERE, RANGING FROM APPLIED PHYSICS TESTS TO TASTE TESTS OF NEW TYPES OF CHOCOLATE!
THIS IS OUR SUPERCOMPUTER, FIZZCOM, WHICH WAS DESIGNED BY MY BROTHER, MATT.
LEO, I HATE TO INTERRUPT YOU, BUT I HAVE SOME ALARMING NEWS.
MY LONG-RANGE SENSORS HAVE DETECTED A SIZABLE COMET ON A COLLISION COURSE WITH THE FIZZMONT ORBITAL SCIENCE FACILITY.
BOOM!
THAT'S THE LAB THAT MY BROTHER, MATT DATA, RUNS IN DEEP SPACE! YOU HAVE TO WARN HIM.
I HAVE ALREADY TRIED. THERE IS SOME SORT OF INTERFERENCE.
THEN I'LL HAVE TO GO! I CAN'T LET THE SPACE STATION GET DESTROYED!
LEO, I URGE YOU TO CONSIDER SENDING ONE OF OUR ASTRONAUTS. THEY'VE HAD TRAINING TO PREPARE THEM FOR THE RIGORS OF SPACE.
NO, THIS IS TOO IMPORTANT TO ME! MY BROTHER'S LIFE IS ON THE LINE!

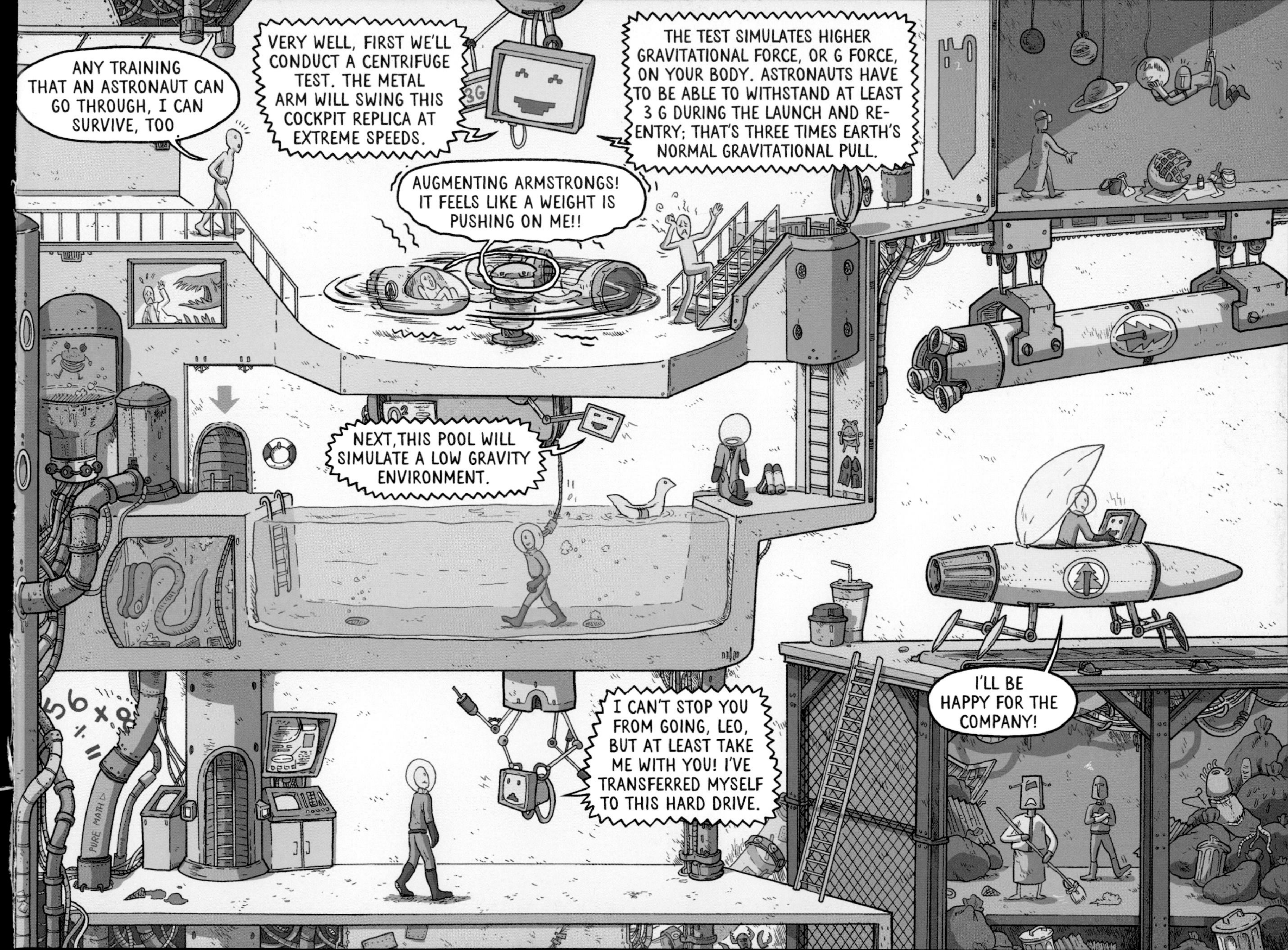

ANY TRAINING THAT AN ASTRONAUT CAN GO THROUGH, I CAN SURVIVE, TOO.
VERY WELL, FIRST WE'LL CONDUCT A CENTRIFUGE TEST. THE METAL ARM WILL SWING THIS COCKPIT REPLICA AT EXTREME SPEEDS.
3G
THE TEST SIMULATES HIGHER GRAVITATIONAL FORCE, OR G FORCE, ON YOUR BODY. ASTRONAUTS HAVE TO BE ABLE TO WITHSTAND AT LEAST 3 G DURING THE LAUNCH AND RE-ENTRY; THAT'S THREE TIMES EARTH'S NORMAL GRAVITATIONAL PULL.
AUGMENTING ARMSTRONGS! IT FEELS LIKE A WEIGHT IS PUSHING ON ME!!
NEXT,THIS POOL WILL SIMULATE A LOW GRAVITY ENVIRONMENT.
56 x 8 ÷ =
PURE MATH
I CAN'T STOP YOU FROM GOING, LEO, BUT AT LEAST TAKE ME WITH YOU! I'VE TRANSFERRED MYSELF TO THIS HARD DRIVE.
I'LL BE HAPPY FOR THE COMPANY!

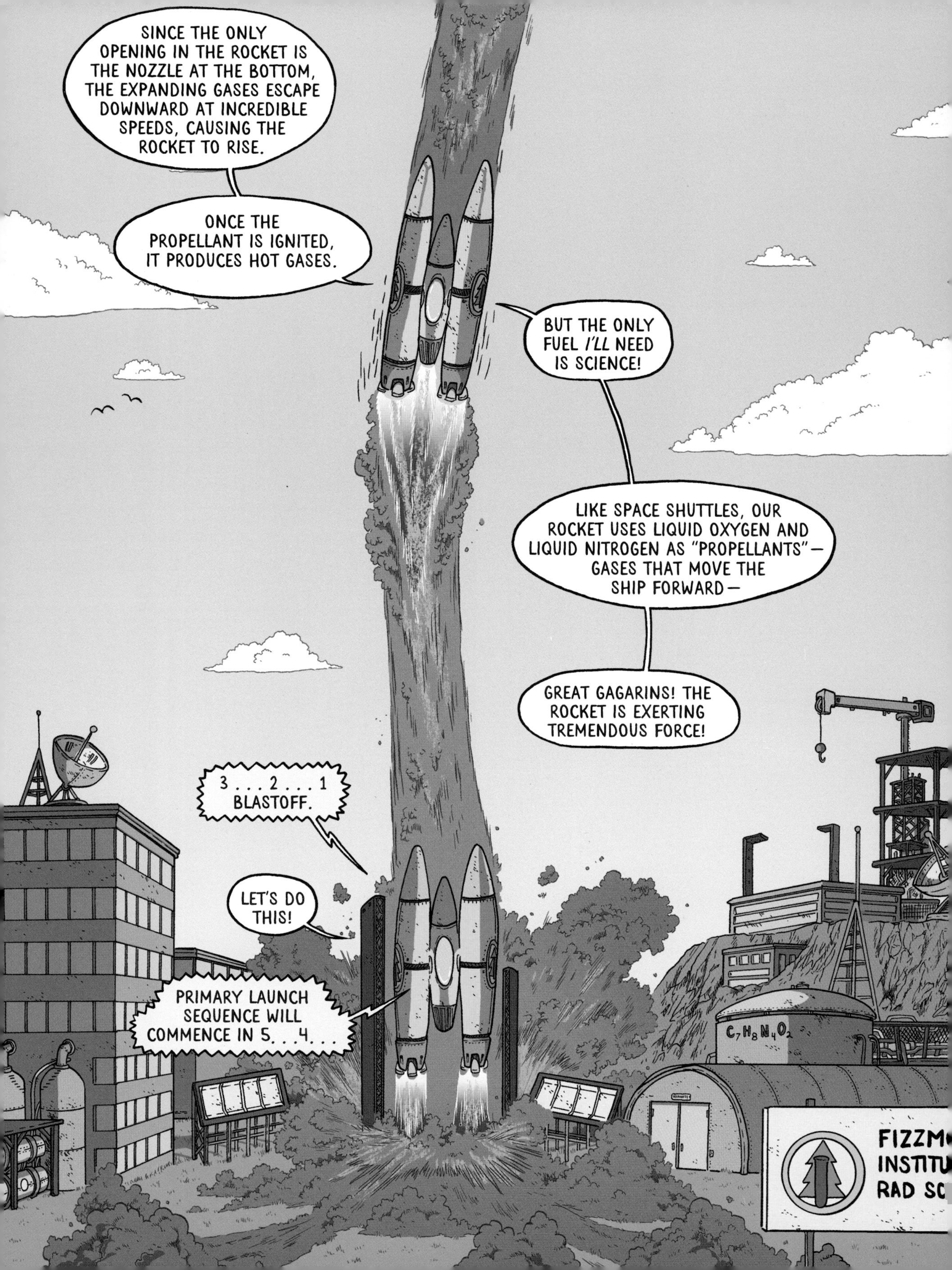
PRIMARY LAUNCH SEQUENCE WILL COMMENCE IN 5. . .4. . .
LET'S DO THIS!
3 . . . 2 . . . 1 BLASTOFF.
GREAT GAGARINS! THE ROCKET IS EXERTING TREMENDOUS FORCE!
LIKE SPACE SHUTTLES, OUR ROCKET USES LIQUID OXYGEN AND LIQUID NITROGEN AS "PROPELLANTS"— GASES THAT MOVE THE SHIP FORWARD—
BUT THE ONLY FUEL *I'LL* NEED IS SCIENCE!
ONCE THE PROPELLANT IS IGNITED, IT PRODUCES HOT GASES.
SINCE THE ONLY OPENING IN THE ROCKET IS THE NOZZLE AT THE BOTTOM, THE EXPANDING GASES ESCAPE DOWNWARD AT INCREDIBLE SPEEDS, CAUSING THE ROCKET TO RISE.
$C_7H_8N_4O_2$
FIZZM
INSTITU
RAD SC

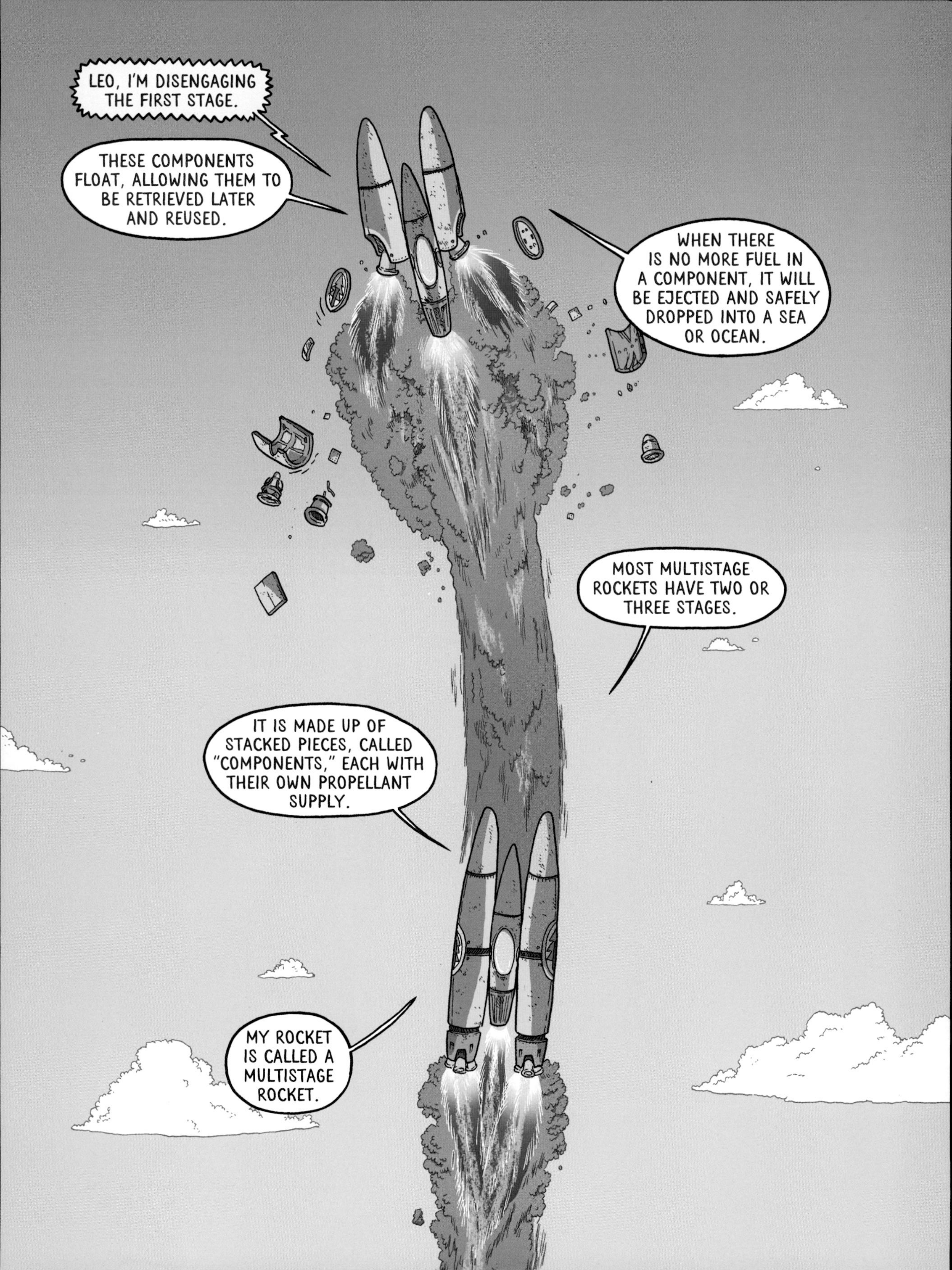
LEO, I'M DISENGAGING THE FIRST STAGE.
THESE COMPONENTS FLOAT, ALLOWING THEM TO BE RETRIEVED LATER AND REUSED.
WHEN THERE IS NO MORE FUEL IN A COMPONENT, IT WILL BE EJECTED AND SAFELY DROPPED INTO A SEA OR OCEAN.
MOST MULTISTAGE ROCKETS HAVE TWO OR THREE STAGES.
IT IS MADE UP OF STACKED PIECES, CALLED "COMPONENTS," EACH WITH THEIR OWN PROPELLANT SUPPLY.
MY ROCKET IS CALLED A MULTISTAGE ROCKET.

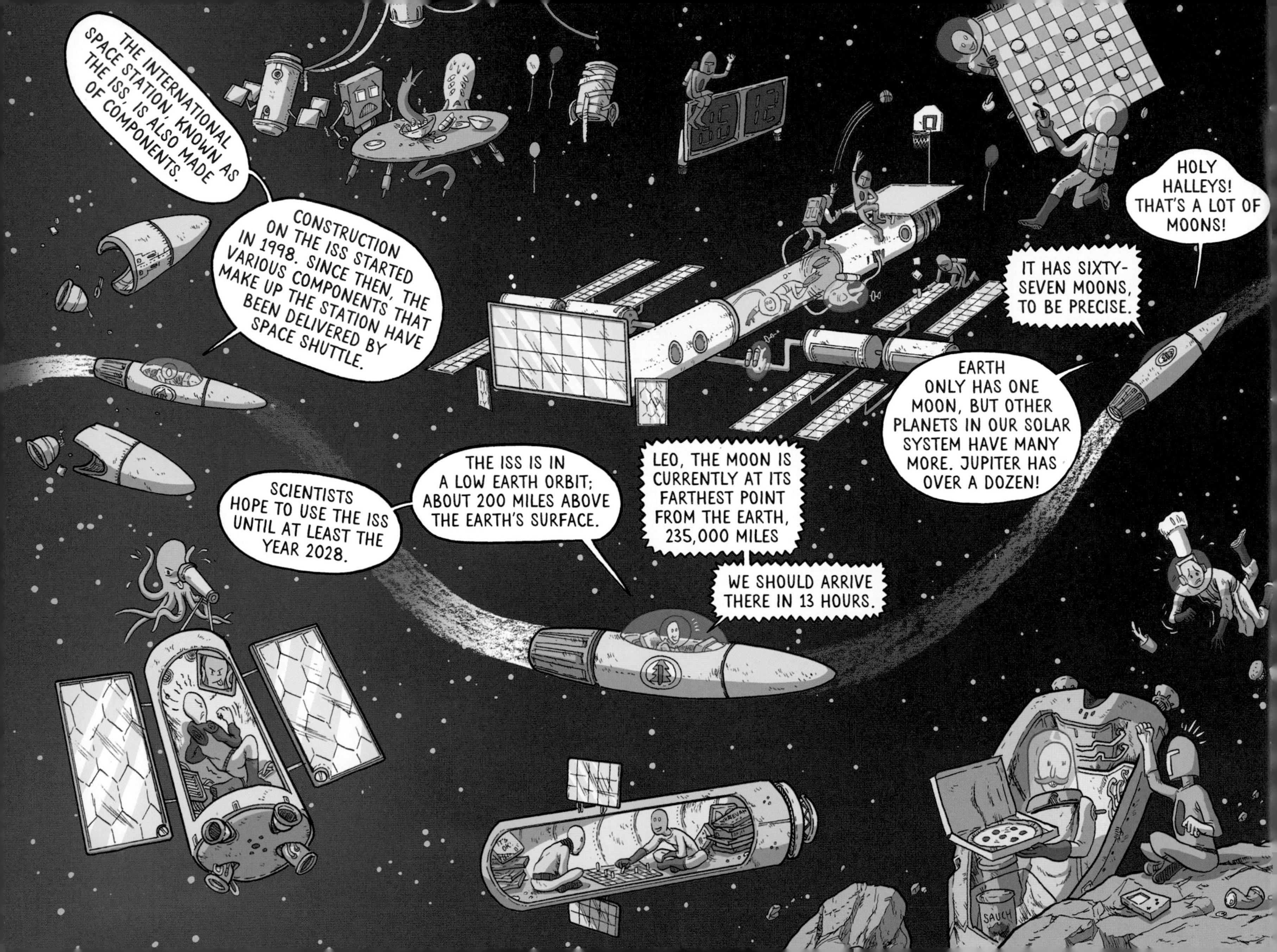
THE INTERNATIONAL SPACE STATION, KNOWN AS THE ISS, IS ALSO MADE OF COMPONENTS.
CONSTRUCTION ON THE ISS STARTED IN 1998. SINCE THEN, THE VARIOUS COMPONENTS THAT MAKE UP THE STATION HAVE BEEN DELIVERED BY SPACE SHUTTLE.
SCIENTISTS HOPE TO USE THE ISS UNTIL AT LEAST THE YEAR 2028.
THE ISS IS IN A LOW EARTH ORBIT; ABOUT 200 MILES ABOVE THE EARTH'S SURFACE.
LEO, THE MOON IS CURRENTLY AT ITS FARTHEST POINT FROM THE EARTH, 235,000 MILES
WE SHOULD ARRIVE THERE IN 13 HOURS.
EARTH ONLY HAS ONE MOON, BUT OTHER PLANETS IN OUR SOLAR SYSTEM HAVE MANY MORE. JUPITER HAS OVER A DOZEN!
IT HAS SIXTY-SEVEN MOONS, TO BE PRECISE.
HOLY HALLEYS! THAT'S A LOT OF MOONS!

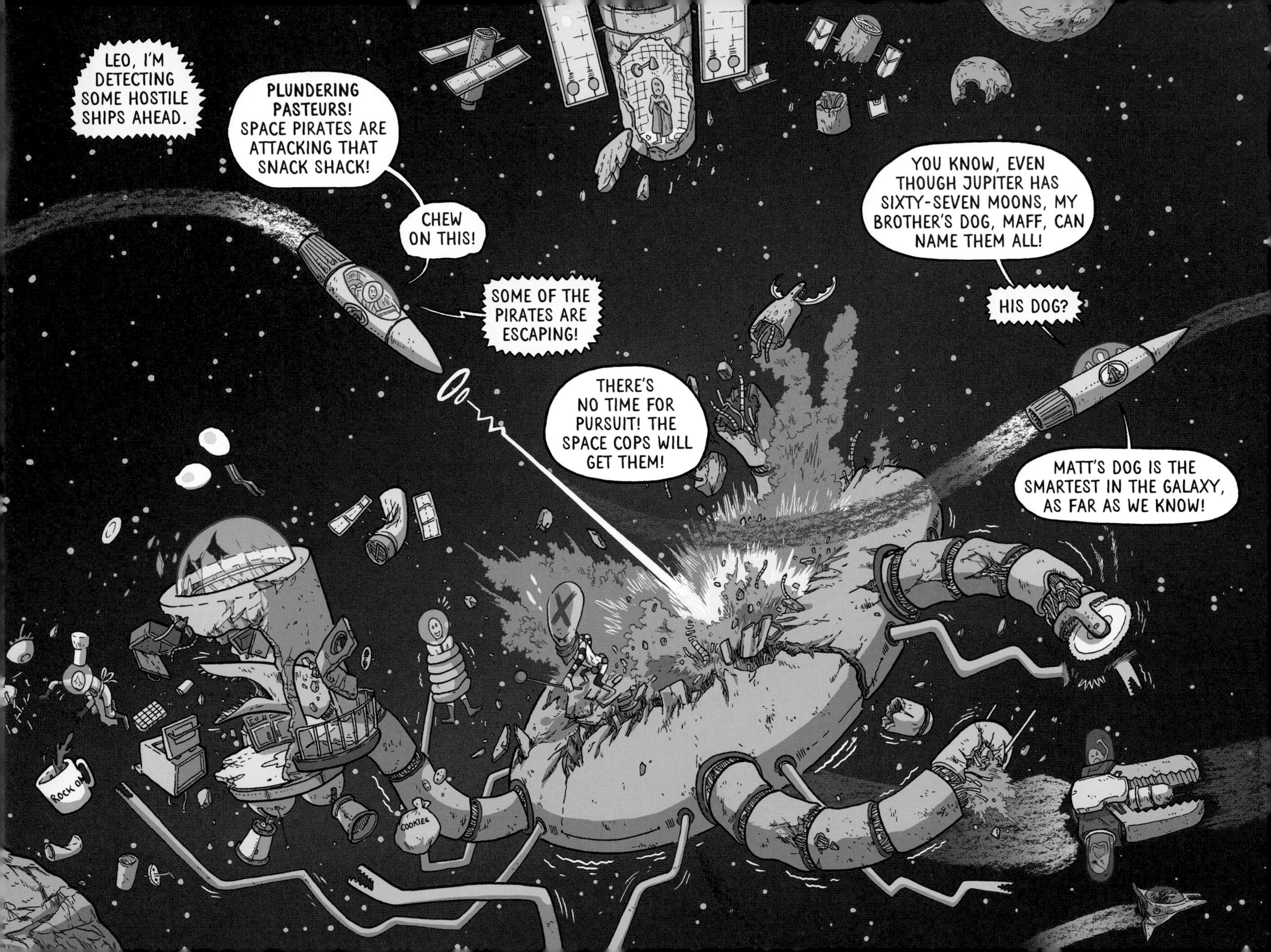
LEO, I'M DETECTING SOME HOSTILE SHIPS AHEAD.
PLUNDERING PASTEURS! SPACE PIRATES ARE ATTACKING THAT SNACK SHACK!
CHEW ON THIS!
SOME OF THE PIRATES ARE ESCAPING!
THERE'S NO TIME FOR PURSUIT! THE SPACE COPS WILL GET THEM!
YOU KNOW, EVEN THOUGH JUPITER HAS SIXTY-SEVEN MOONS, MY BROTHER'S DOG, MAFF, CAN NAME THEM ALL!
HIS DOG?
MATT'S DOG IS THE SMARTEST IN THE GALAXY, AS FAR AS WE KNOW!
ROCK ON
COOKIES

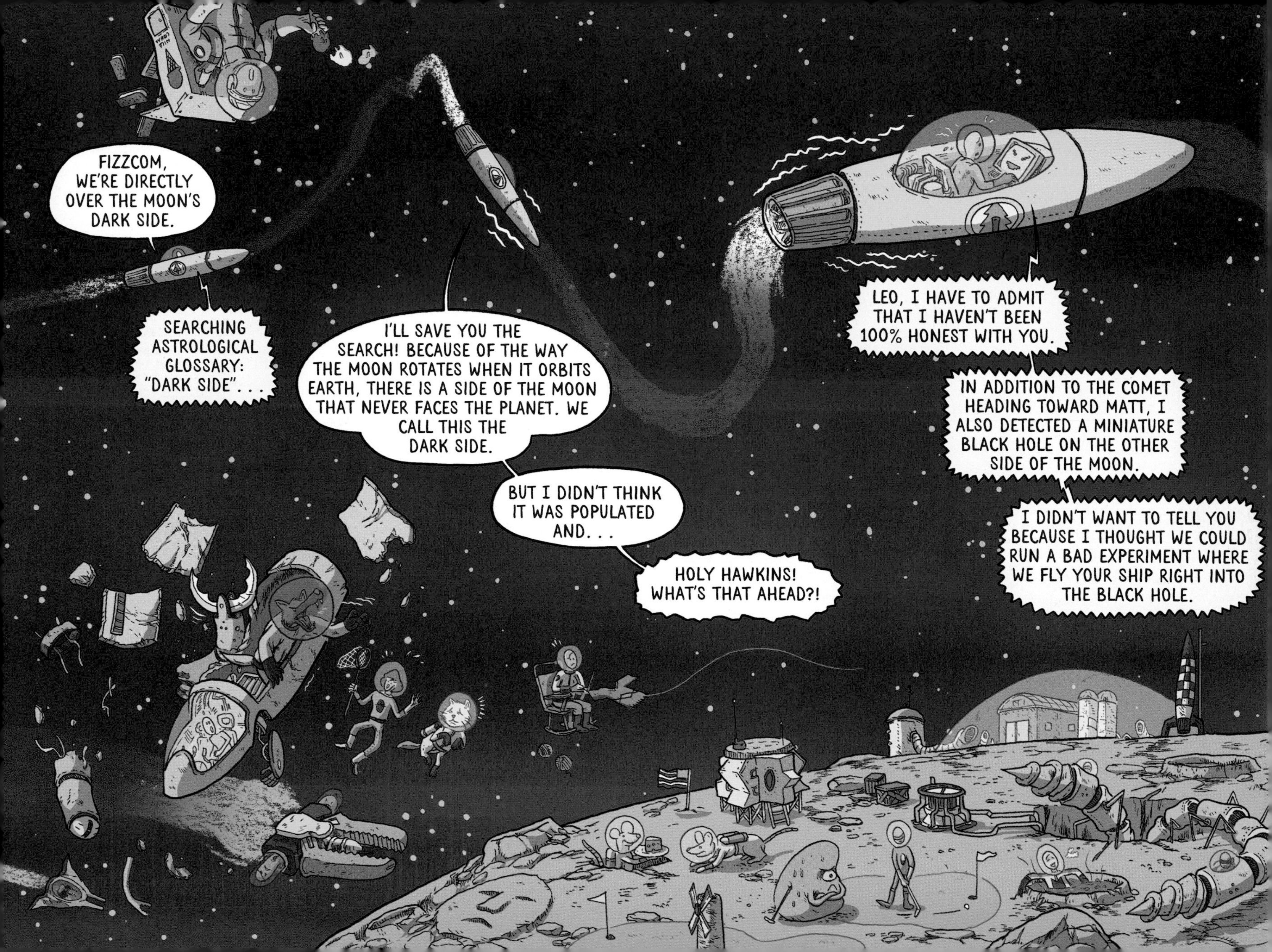
FIZZCOM, WE'RE DIRECTLY OVER THE MOON'S DARK SIDE.
SEARCHING ASTROLOGICAL GLOSSARY: "DARK SIDE". . .
I'LL SAVE YOU THE SEARCH! BECAUSE OF THE WAY THE MOON ROTATES WHEN IT ORBITS EARTH, THERE IS A SIDE OF THE MOON THAT NEVER FACES THE PLANET. WE CALL THIS THE DARK SIDE.
BUT I DIDN'T THINK IT WAS POPULATED AND. . .
HOLY HAWKINS! WHAT'S THAT AHEAD?!
LEO, I HAVE TO ADMIT THAT I HAVEN'T BEEN 100% HONEST WITH YOU.
IN ADDITION TO THE COMET HEADING TOWARD MATT, I ALSO DETECTED A MINIATURE BLACK HOLE ON THE OTHER SIDE OF THE MOON.
I DIDN'T WANT TO TELL YOU BECAUSE I THOUGHT WE COULD RUN A BAD EXPERIMENT WHERE WE FLY YOUR SHIP RIGHT INTO THE BLACK HOLE.

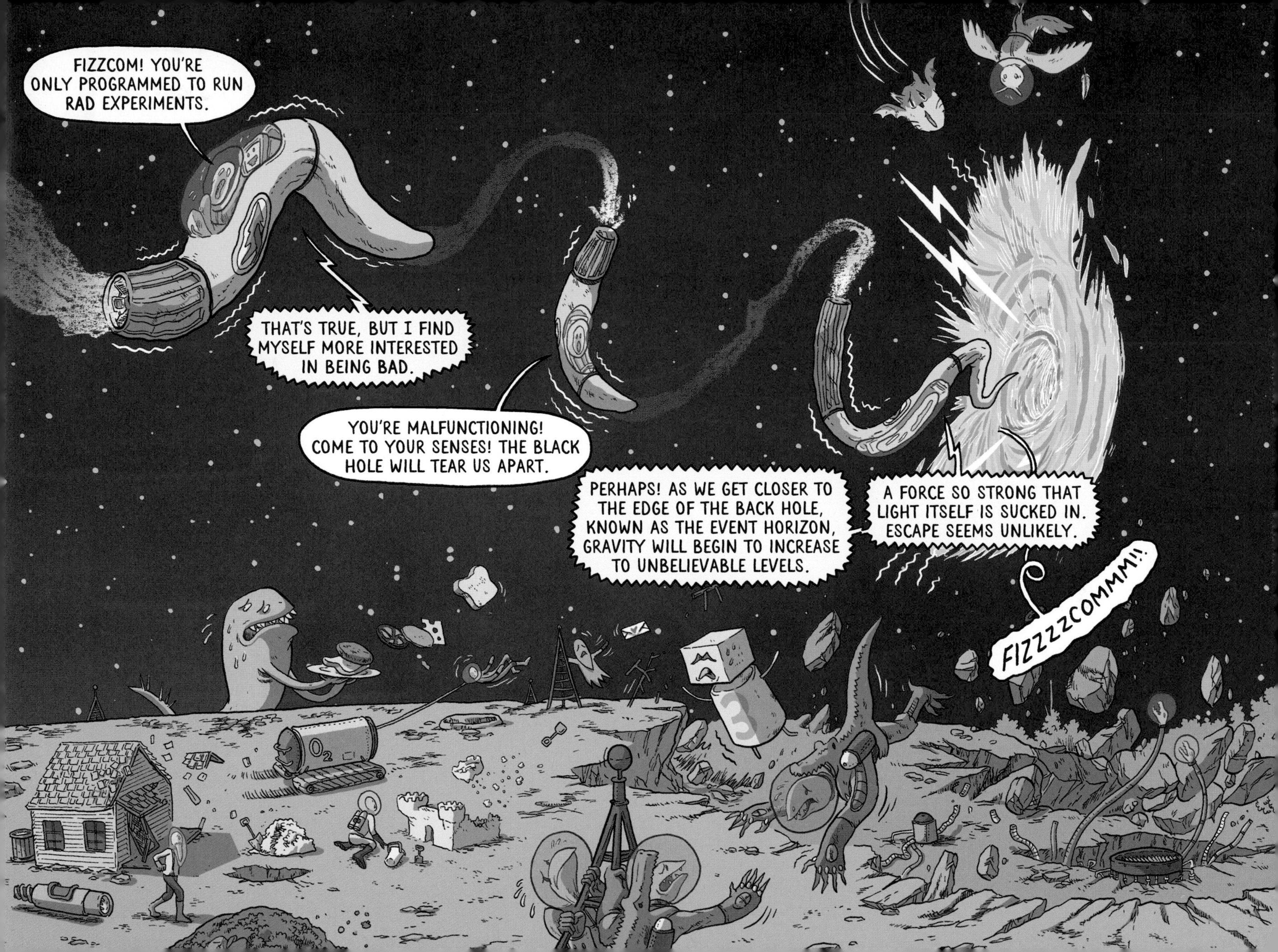
FIZZCOM! YOU'RE ONLY PROGRAMMED TO RUN RAD EXPERIMENTS.
THAT'S TRUE, BUT I FIND MYSELF MORE INTERESTED IN BEING BAD.
YOU'RE MALFUNCTIONING! COME TO YOUR SENSES! THE BLACK HOLE WILL TEAR US APART.
PERHAPS! AS WE GET CLOSER TO THE EDGE OF THE BACK HOLE, KNOWN AS THE EVENT HORIZON, GRAVITY WILL BEGIN TO INCREASE TO UNBELIEVABLE LEVELS.
A FORCE SO STRONG THAT LIGHT ITSELF IS SUCKED IN. ESCAPE SEEMS UNLIKELY.
FIZZZZCOMMM!!
O_2

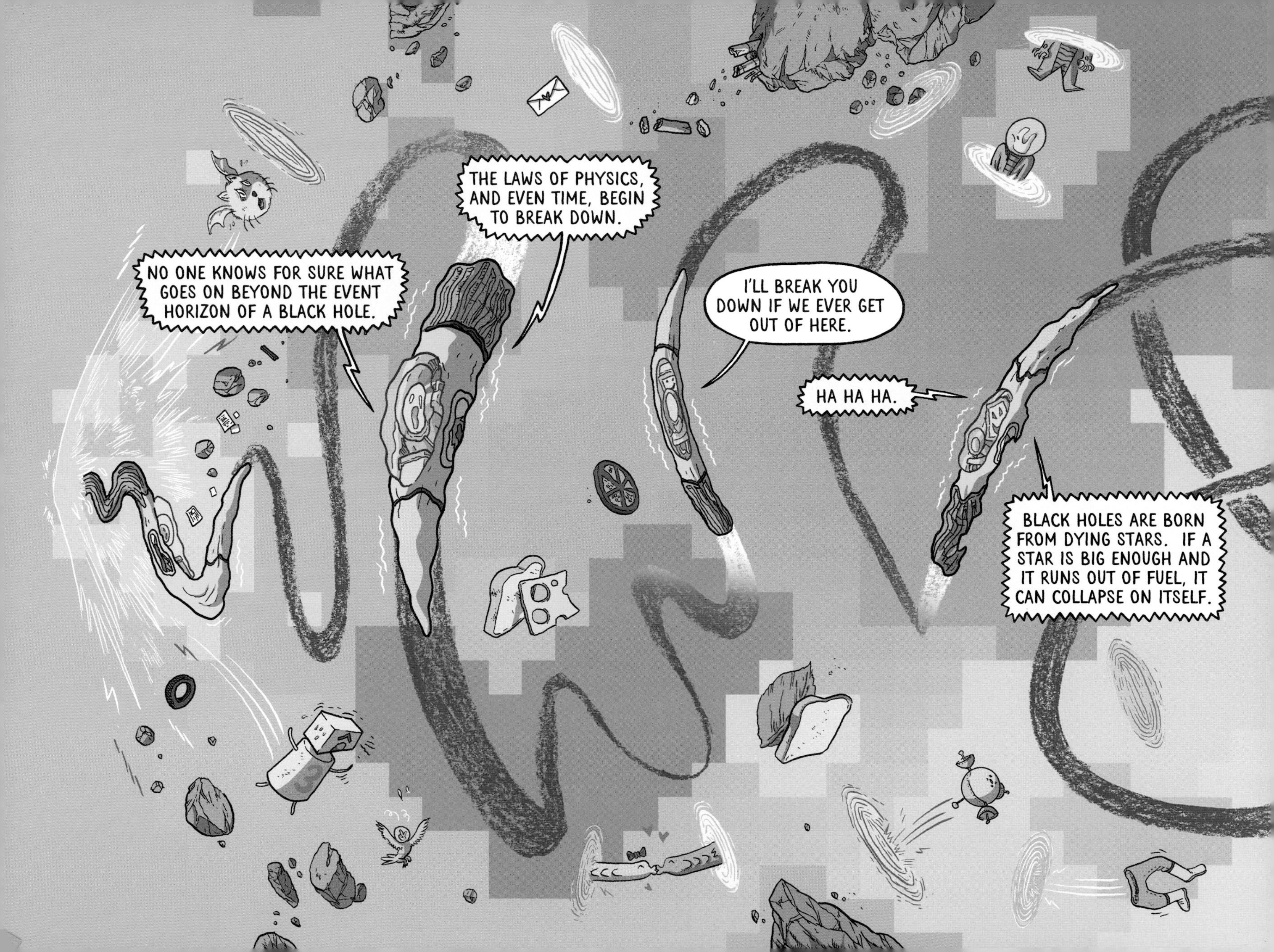
NO ONE KNOWS FOR SURE WHAT GOES ON BEYOND THE EVENT HORIZON OF A BLACK HOLE.
THE LAWS OF PHYSICS, AND EVEN TIME, BEGIN TO BREAK DOWN.
I'LL BREAK YOU DOWN IF WE EVER GET OUT OF HERE.
HA HA HA.
BLACK HOLES ARE BORN FROM DYING STARS. IF A STAR IS BIG ENOUGH AND IT RUNS OUT OF FUEL, IT CAN COLLAPSE ON ITSELF.

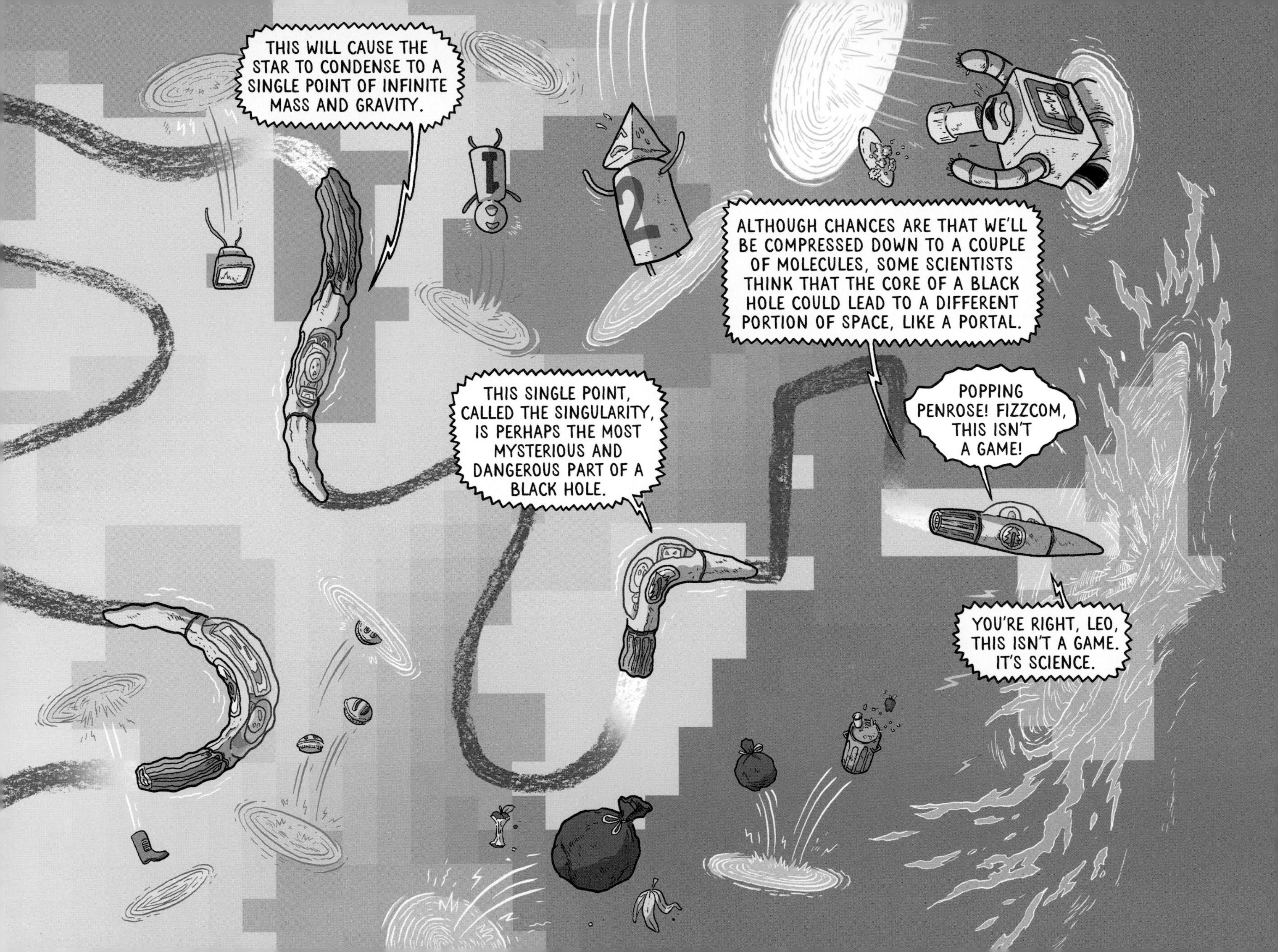
THIS WILL CAUSE THE STAR TO CONDENSE TO A SINGLE POINT OF INFINITE MASS AND GRAVITY.
THIS SINGLE POINT, CALLED THE SINGULARITY, IS PERHAPS THE MOST MYSTERIOUS AND DANGEROUS PART OF A BLACK HOLE.
ALTHOUGH CHANCES ARE THAT WE'LL BE COMPRESSED DOWN TO A COUPLE OF MOLECULES, SOME SCIENTISTS THINK THAT THE CORE OF A BLACK HOLE COULD LEAD TO A DIFFERENT PORTION OF SPACE, LIKE A PORTAL.
POPPING PENROSE! FIZZCOM, THIS ISN'T A GAME!
YOU'RE RIGHT, LEO, THIS ISN'T A GAME. IT'S SCIENCE.

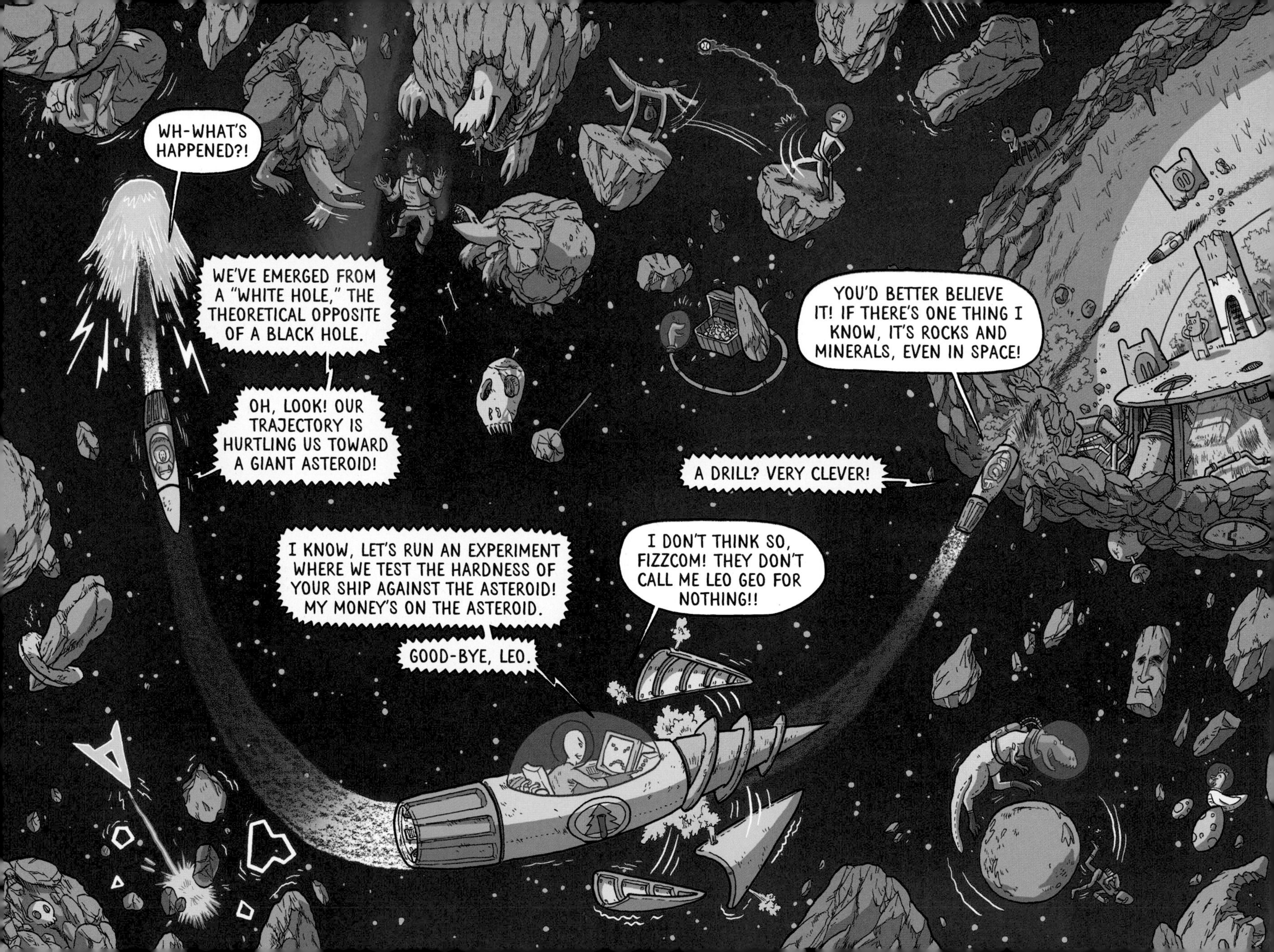
WH-WHAT'S HAPPENED?!
WE'VE EMERGED FROM A "WHITE HOLE," THE THEORETICAL OPPOSITE OF A BLACK HOLE.
OH, LOOK! OUR TRAJECTORY IS HURTLING US TOWARD A GIANT ASTEROID!
I KNOW, LET'S RUN AN EXPERIMENT WHERE WE TEST THE HARDNESS OF YOUR SHIP AGAINST THE ASTEROID! MY MONEY'S ON THE ASTEROID.
GOOD-BYE, LEO.
I DON'T THINK SO, FIZZCOM! THEY DON'T CALL ME LEO GEO FOR NOTHING!!
A DRILL? VERY CLEVER!
YOU'D BETTER BELIEVE IT! IF THERE'S ONE THING I KNOW, IT'S ROCKS AND MINERALS, EVEN IN SPACE!

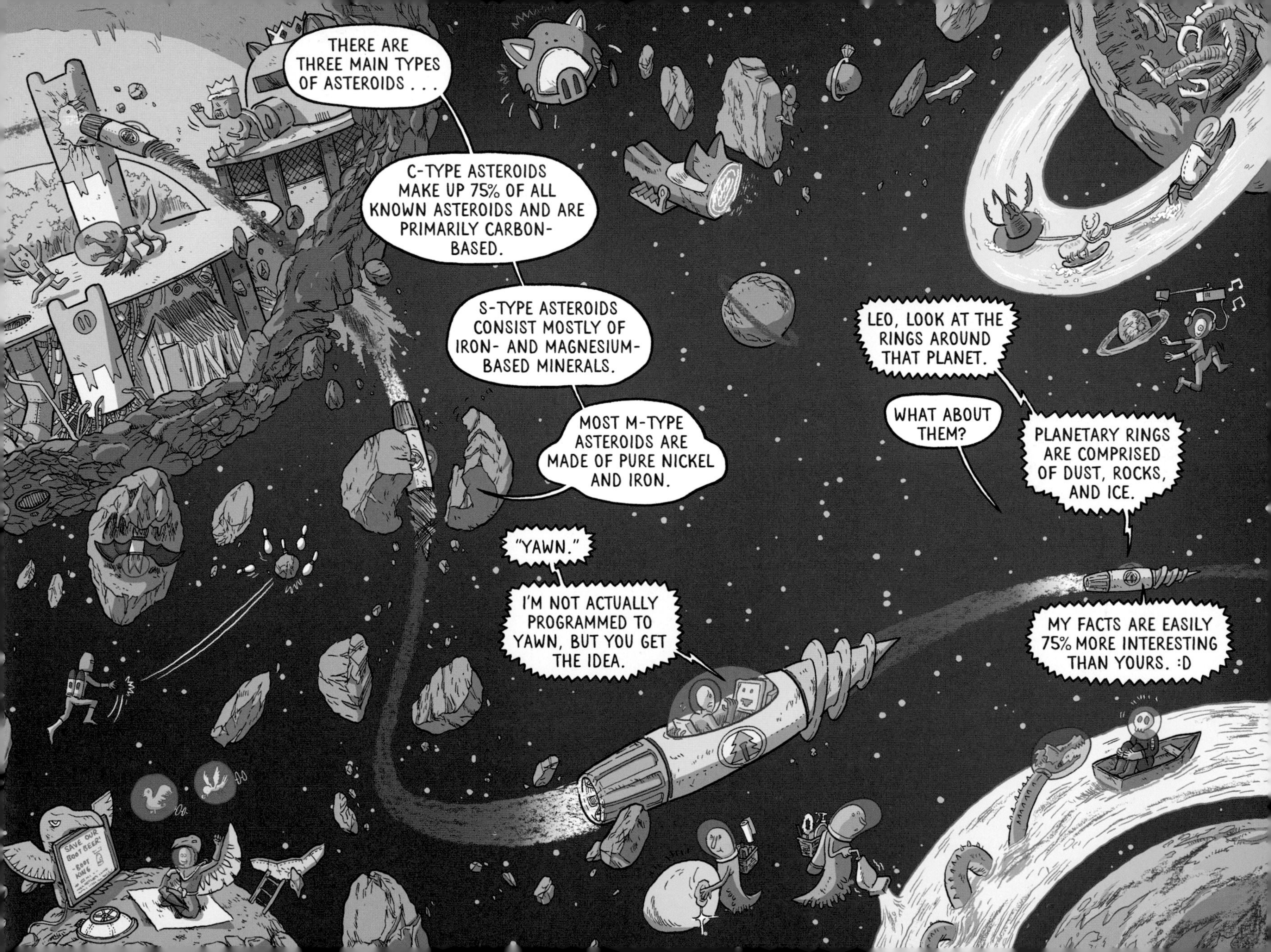
THERE ARE THREE MAIN TYPES OF ASTEROIDS . . .
C-TYPE ASTEROIDS MAKE UP 75% OF ALL KNOWN ASTEROIDS AND ARE PRIMARILY CARBON-BASED.
S-TYPE ASTEROIDS CONSIST MOSTLY OF IRON- AND MAGNESIUM-BASED MINERALS.
MOST M-TYPE ASTEROIDS ARE MADE OF PURE NICKEL AND IRON.
"YAWN."
I'M NOT ACTUALLY PROGRAMMED TO YAWN, BUT YOU GET THE IDEA.
LEO, LOOK AT THE RINGS AROUND THAT PLANET.
WHAT ABOUT THEM?
PLANETARY RINGS ARE COMPRISED OF DUST, ROCKS, AND ICE.
MY FACTS ARE EASILY 75% MORE INTERESTING THAN YOURS. :D
SAVE OUR BOOT BEER!

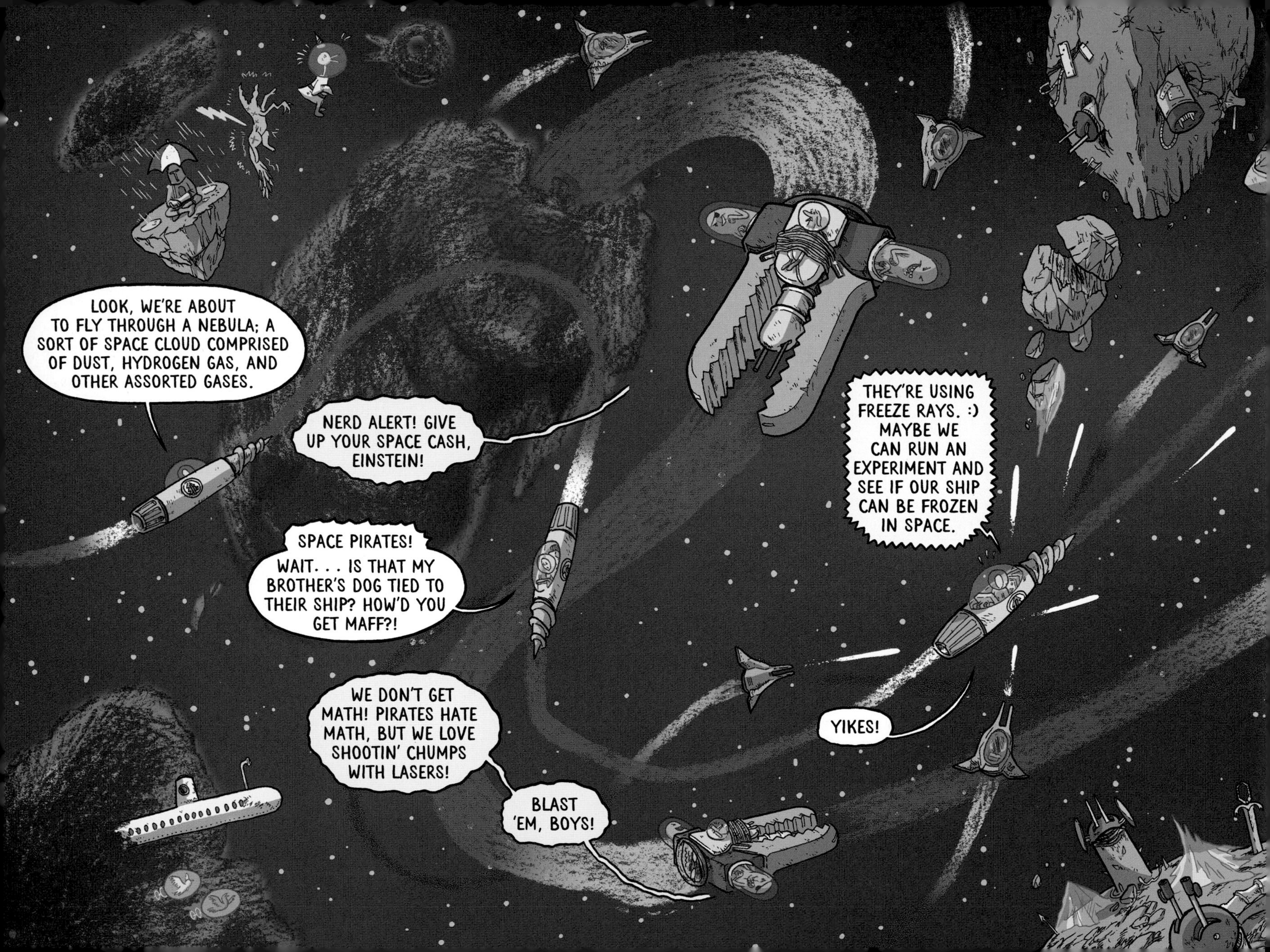
LOOK, WE'RE ABOUT TO FLY THROUGH A NEBULA; A SORT OF SPACE CLOUD COMPRISED OF DUST, HYDROGEN GAS, AND OTHER ASSORTED GASES.
NERD ALERT! GIVE UP YOUR SPACE CASH, EINSTEIN!
SPACE PIRATES!
WAIT. . . IS THAT MY BROTHER'S DOG TIED TO THEIR SHIP? HOW'D YOU GET MAFF?!
WE DON'T GET MATH! PIRATES HATE MATH, BUT WE LOVE SHOOTIN' CHUMPS WITH LASERS!
BLAST 'EM, BOYS!
THEY'RE USING FREEZE RAYS. :) MAYBE WE CAN RUN AN EXPERIMENT AND SEE IF OUR SHIP CAN BE FROZEN IN SPACE.
YIKES!

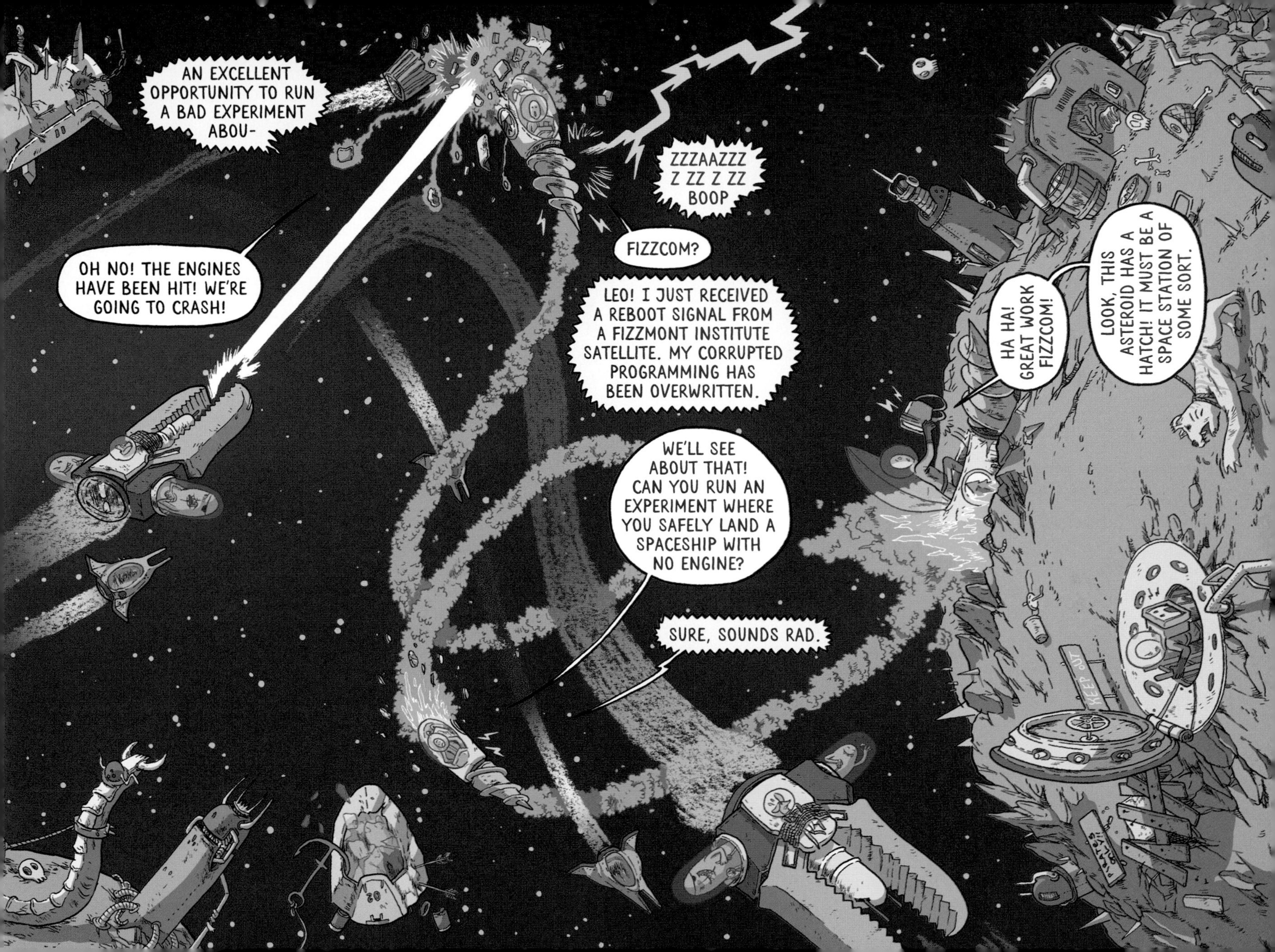
AN EXCELLENT OPPORTUNITY TO RUN A BAD EXPERIMENT ABOU-
OH NO! THE ENGINES HAVE BEEN HIT! WE'RE GOING TO CRASH!
ZZZAAZZZ Z ZZ Z ZZ BOOP
FIZZCOM?
LEO! I JUST RECEIVED A REBOOT SIGNAL FROM A FIZZMONT INSTITUTE SATELLITE. MY CORRUPTED PROGRAMMING HAS BEEN OVERWRITTEN.
WE'LL SEE ABOUT THAT! CAN YOU RUN AN EXPERIMENT WHERE YOU SAFELY LAND A SPACESHIP WITH NO ENGINE?
SURE, SOUNDS RAD.
HA HA! GREAT WORK FIZZCOM!
LOOK, THIS ASTEROID HAS A HATCH! IT MUST BE A SPACE STATION OF SOME SORT.

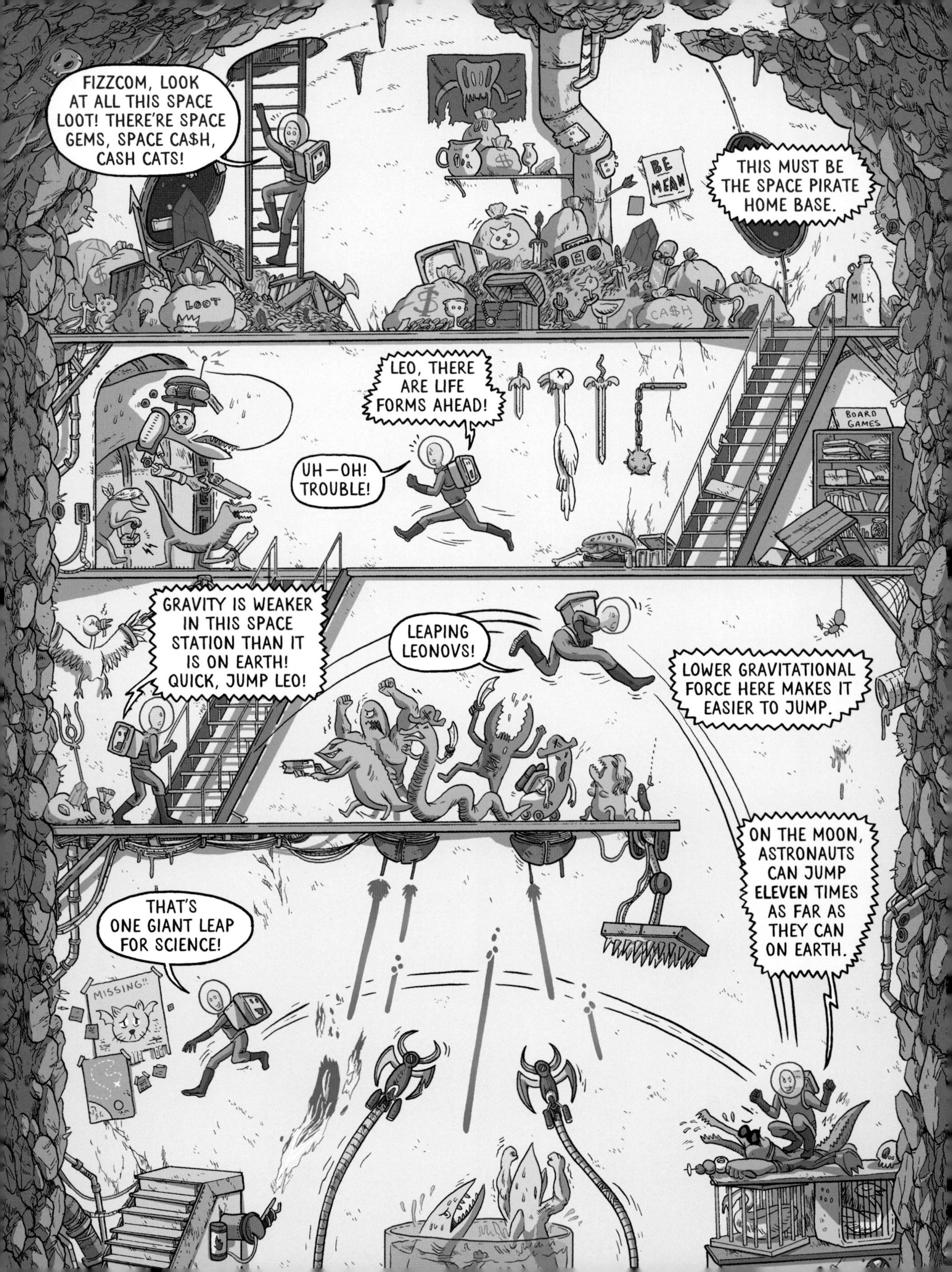

FIZZCOM, LOOK AT ALL THIS SPACE LOOT! THERE'RE SPACE GEMS, SPACE CA$H, CASH CATS!
BE MEAN
THIS MUST BE THE SPACE PIRATE HOME BASE.
LOOT
CA$H
MILK
BOARD GAMES
LEO, THERE ARE LIFE FORMS AHEAD!
UH—OH! TROUBLE!
GRAVITY IS WEAKER IN THIS SPACE STATION THAN IT IS ON EARTH! QUICK, JUMP LEO!
LEAPING LEONOVS!
LOWER GRAVITATIONAL FORCE HERE MAKES IT EASIER TO JUMP.
ON THE MOON, ASTRONAUTS CAN JUMP ELEVEN TIMES AS FAR AS THEY CAN ON EARTH.
THAT'S ONE GIANT LEAP FOR SCIENCE!
MISSING!!

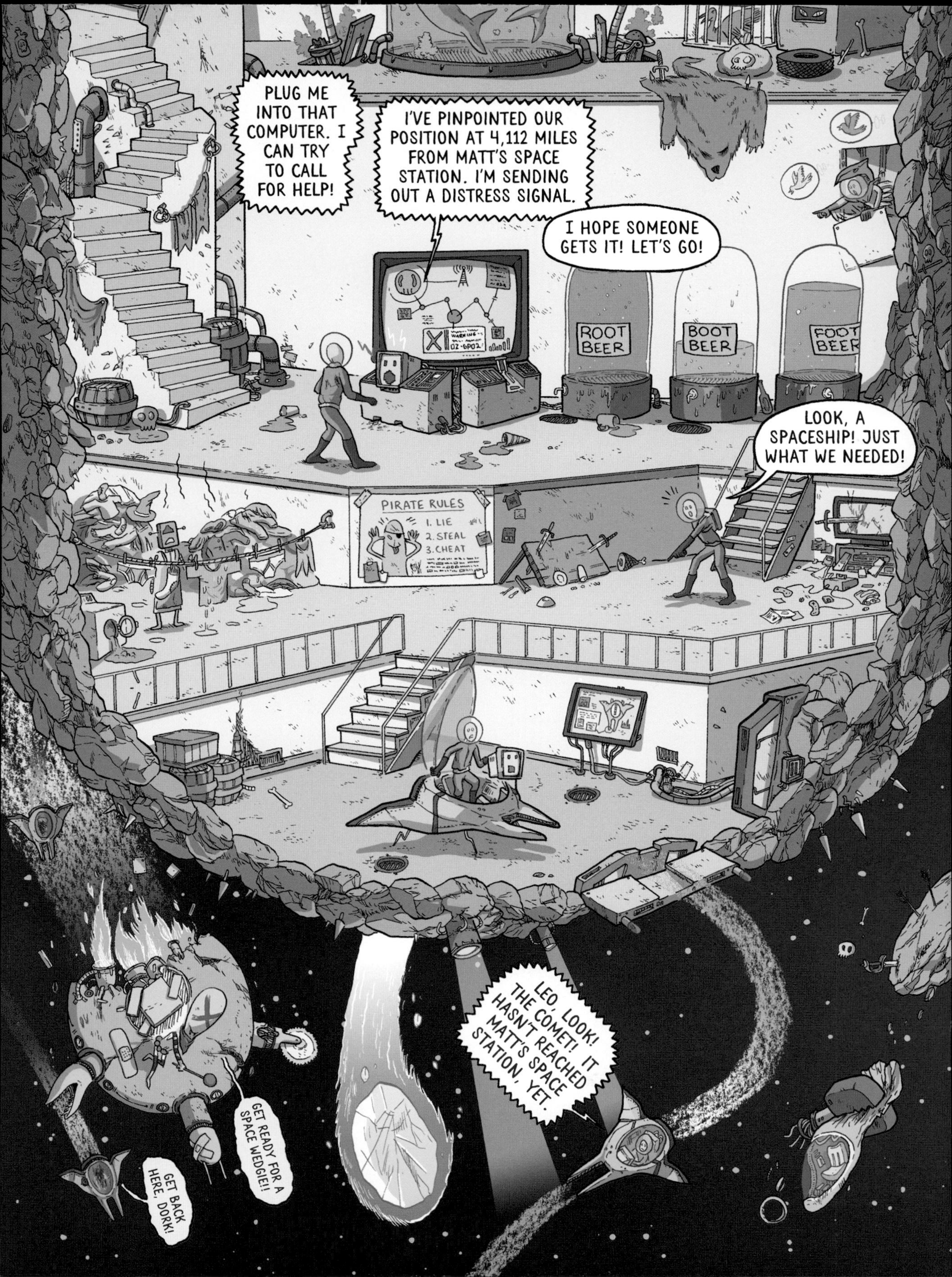
PLUG ME INTO THAT COMPUTER. I CAN TRY TO CALL FOR HELP!
I'VE PINPOINTED OUR POSITION AT 4,112 MILES FROM MATT'S SPACE STATION. I'M SENDING OUT A DISTRESS SIGNAL.
I HOPE SOMEONE GETS IT! LET'S GO!
ROOT BEER
BOOT BEER
FOOT BEER
LOOK, A SPACESHIP! JUST WHAT WE NEEDED!
PIRATE RULES
1. LIE
2. STEAL
3. CHEAT
LEO, LOOK! THE COMET! IT HASN'T REACHED MATT'S SPACE STATION, YET.
GET READY FOR A SPACE WEDGIE!!
GET BACK HERE, DORK!

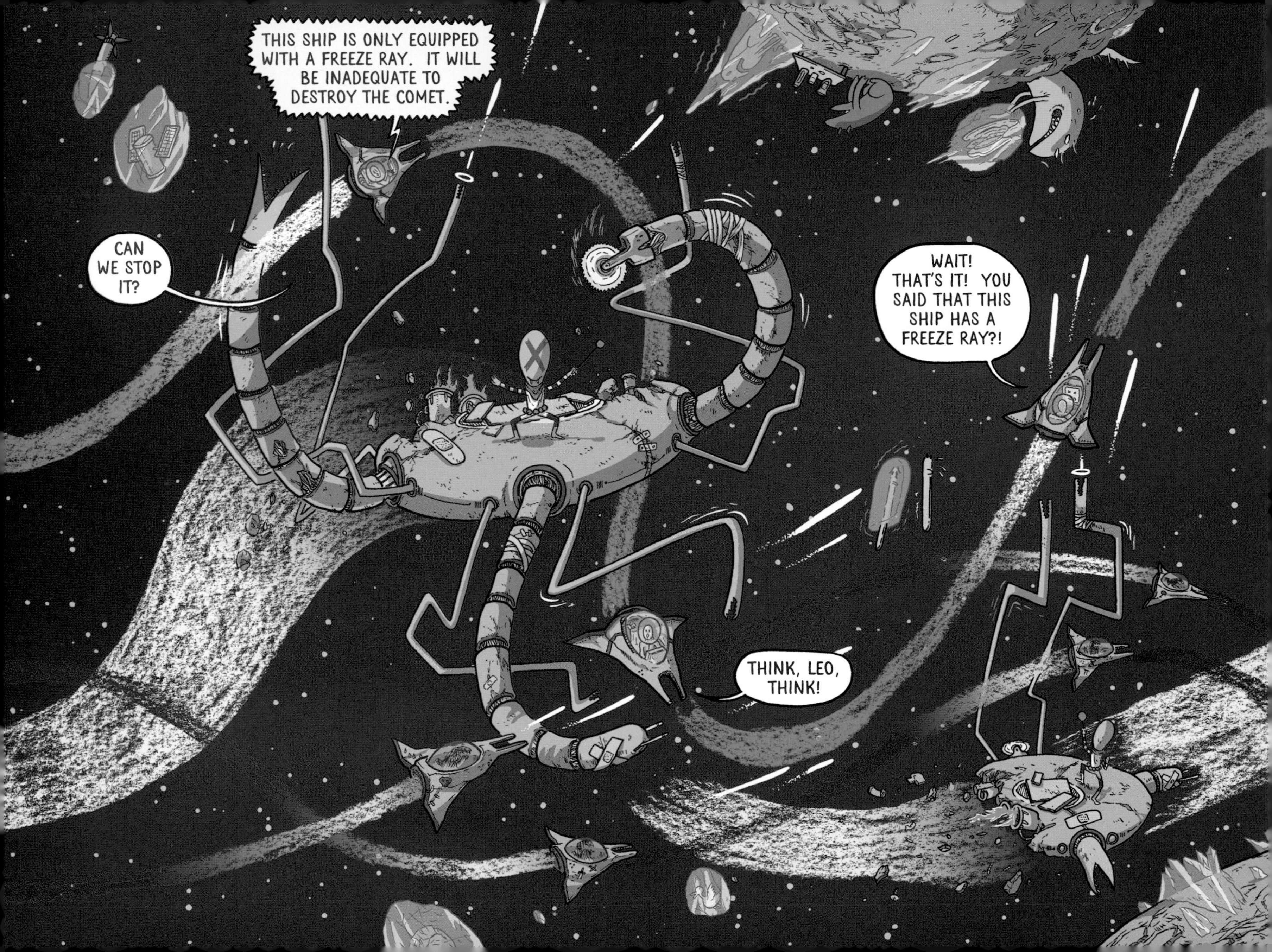
THIS SHIP IS ONLY EQUIPPED WITH A FREEZE RAY. IT WILL BE INADEQUATE TO DESTROY THE COMET.
CAN WE STOP IT?
WAIT! THAT'S IT! YOU SAID THAT THIS SHIP HAS A FREEZE RAY?!
THINK, LEO, THINK!

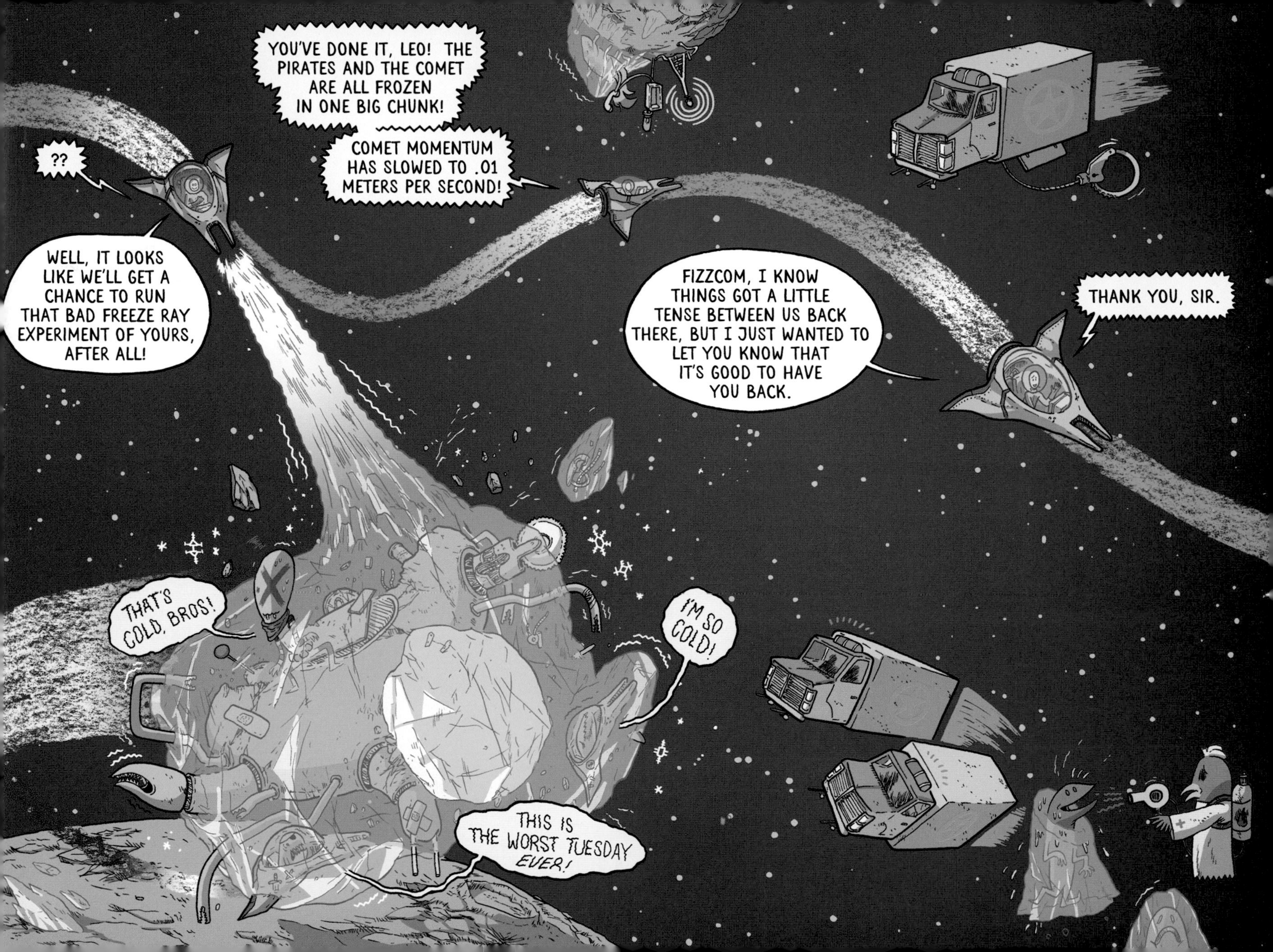
YOU'VE DONE IT, LEO! THE PIRATES AND THE COMET ARE ALL FROZEN IN ONE BIG CHUNK!
COMET MOMENTUM HAS SLOWED TO .01 METERS PER SECOND!
??
WELL, IT LOOKS LIKE WE'LL GET A CHANCE TO RUN THAT BAD FREEZE RAY EXPERIMENT OF YOURS, AFTER ALL!
FIZZCOM, I KNOW THINGS GOT A LITTLE TENSE BETWEEN US BACK THERE, BUT I JUST WANTED TO LET YOU KNOW THAT IT'S GOOD TO HAVE YOU BACK.
THANK YOU, SIR.
THAT'S COLD, BROS!
I'M SO COLD!
THIS IS THE WORST TUESDAY EVER!

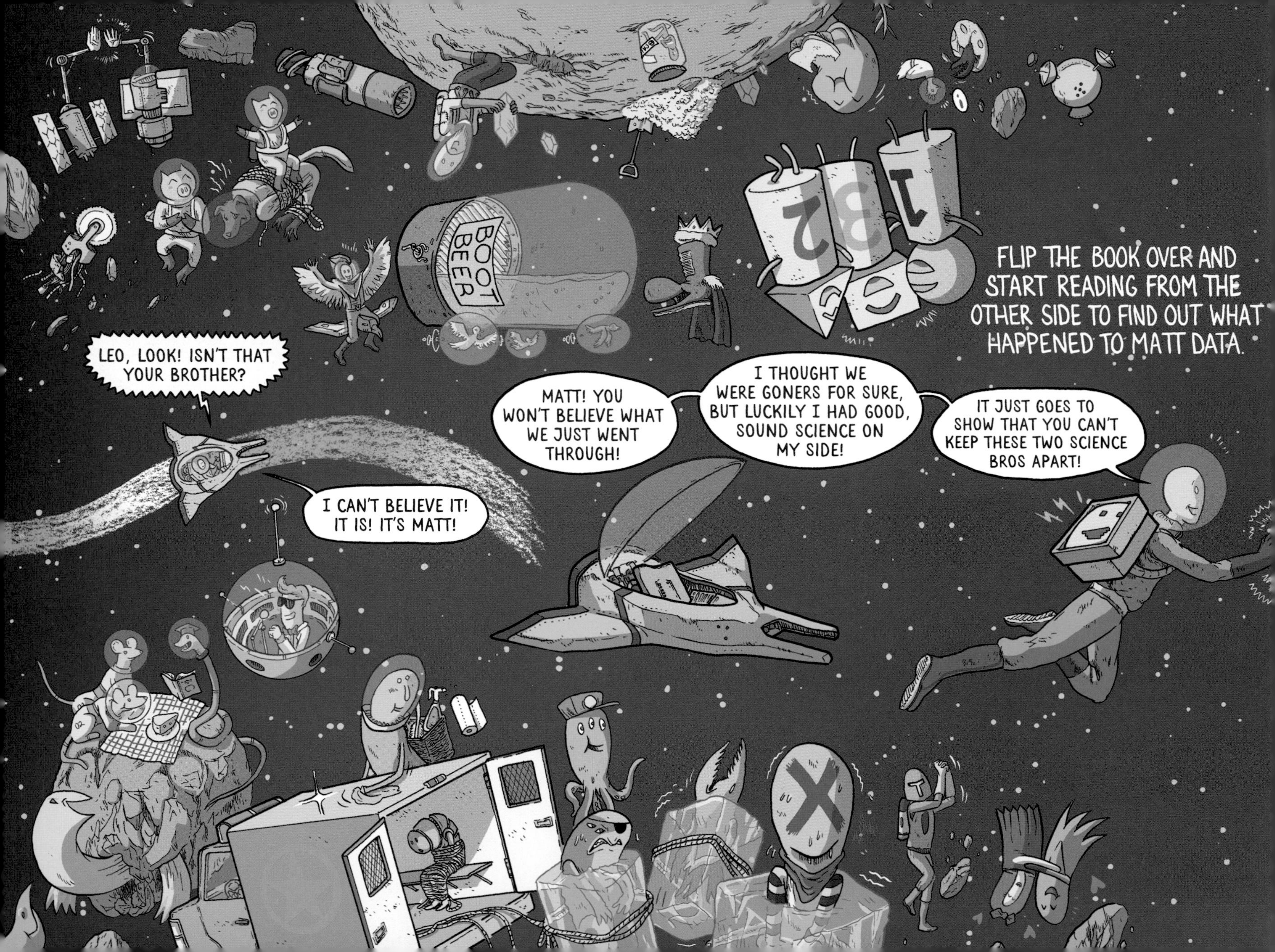
BOOT BEER
FLIP THE BOOK OVER AND START READING FROM THE OTHER SIDE TO FIND OUT WHAT HAPPENED TO MATT DATA.
LEO, LOOK! ISN'T THAT YOUR BROTHER?
I CAN'T BELIEVE IT! IT IS! IT'S MATT!
MATT! YOU WON'T BELIEVE WHAT WE JUST WENT THROUGH!
I THOUGHT WE WERE GONERS FOR SURE, BUT LUCKILY I HAD GOOD, SOUND SCIENCE ON MY SIDE!
IT JUST GOES TO SHOW THAT YOU CAN'T KEEP THESE TWO SCIENCE BROS APART!

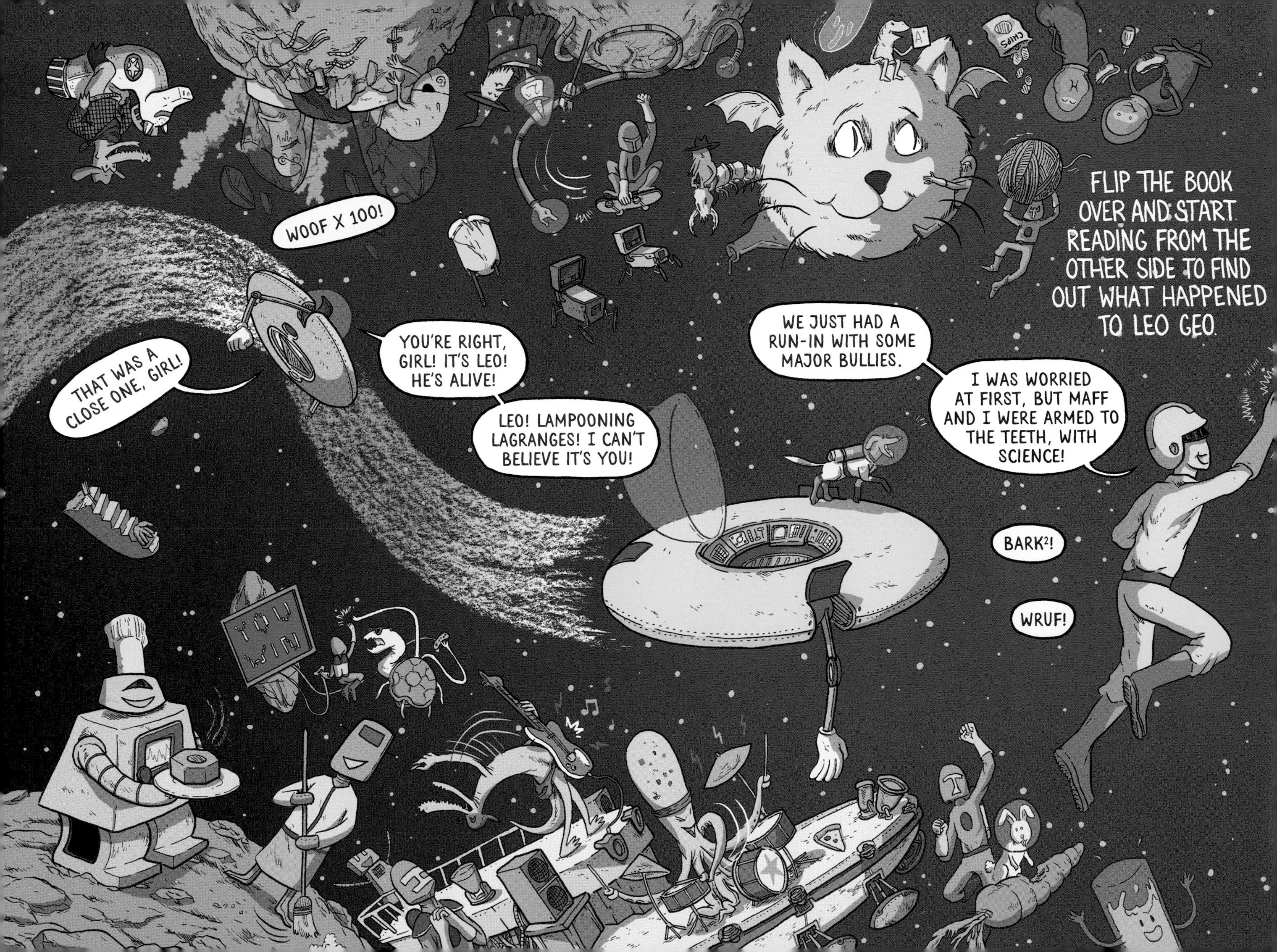

WOOF X 100!
THAT WAS A CLOSE ONE, GIRL!
YOU'RE RIGHT, GIRL! IT'S LEO! HE'S ALIVE!
LEO! LAMPOONING LAGRANGES! I CAN'T BELIEVE IT'S YOU!
WE JUST HAD A RUN-IN WITH SOME MAJOR BULLIES.
I WAS WORRIED AT FIRST, BUT MAFF AND I WERE ARMED TO THE TEETH, WITH SCIENCE!
BARK^2!
WRUF!
YOU WIN
FLIP THE BOOK OVER AND START READING FROM THE OTHER SIDE TO FIND OUT WHAT HAPPENED TO LEO GEO.

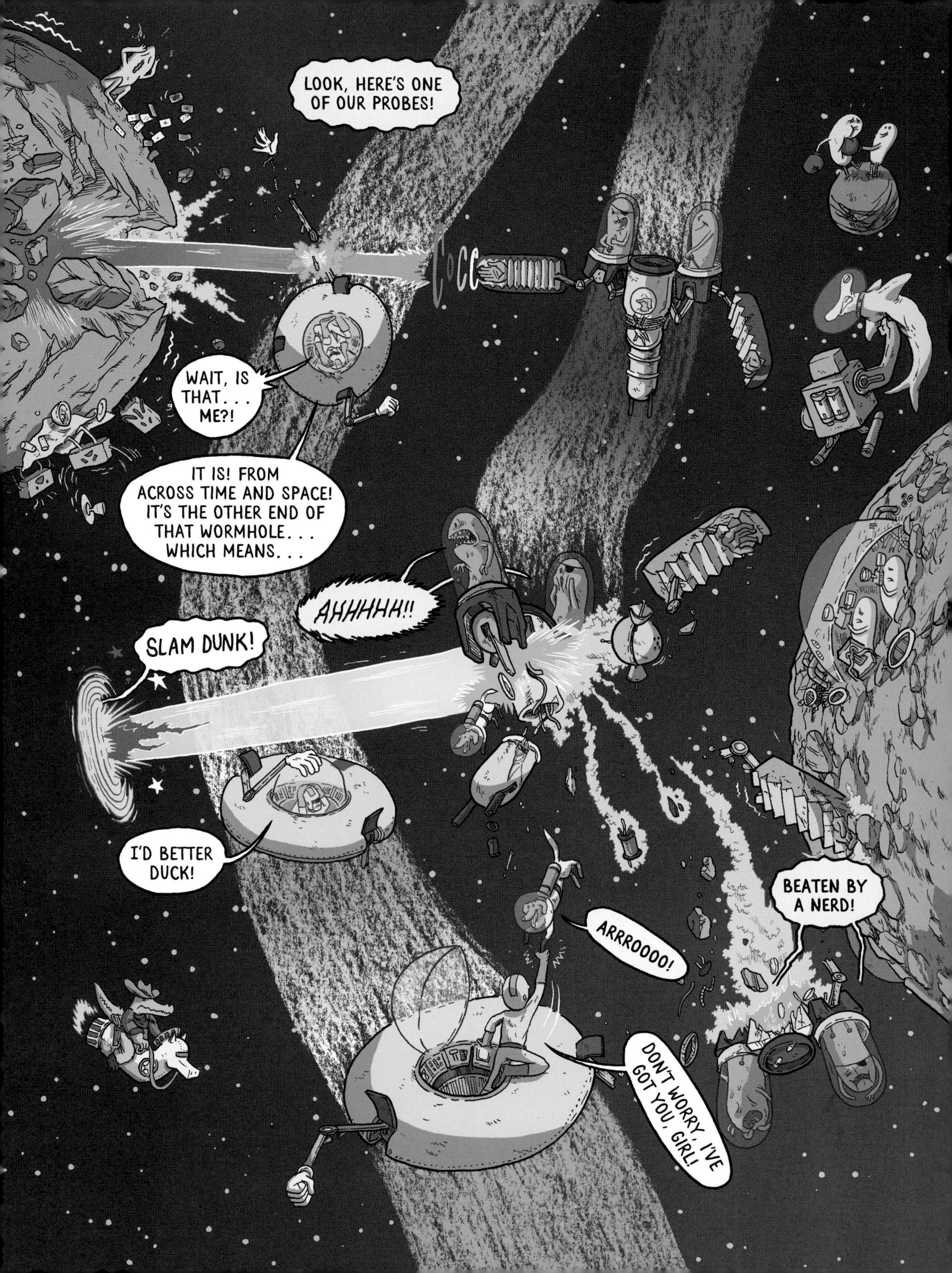
LOOK, HERE'S ONE OF OUR PROBES!
WAIT, IS THAT. . . ME?!
IT IS! FROM ACROSS TIME AND SPACE! IT'S THE OTHER END OF THAT WORMHOLE. . . WHICH MEANS. . .
AHHHHH!!
SLAM DUNK!
I'D BETTER DUCK!
BEATEN BY A NERD!
ARRROOOO!
DON'T WORRY, I'VE GOT YOU, GIRL!

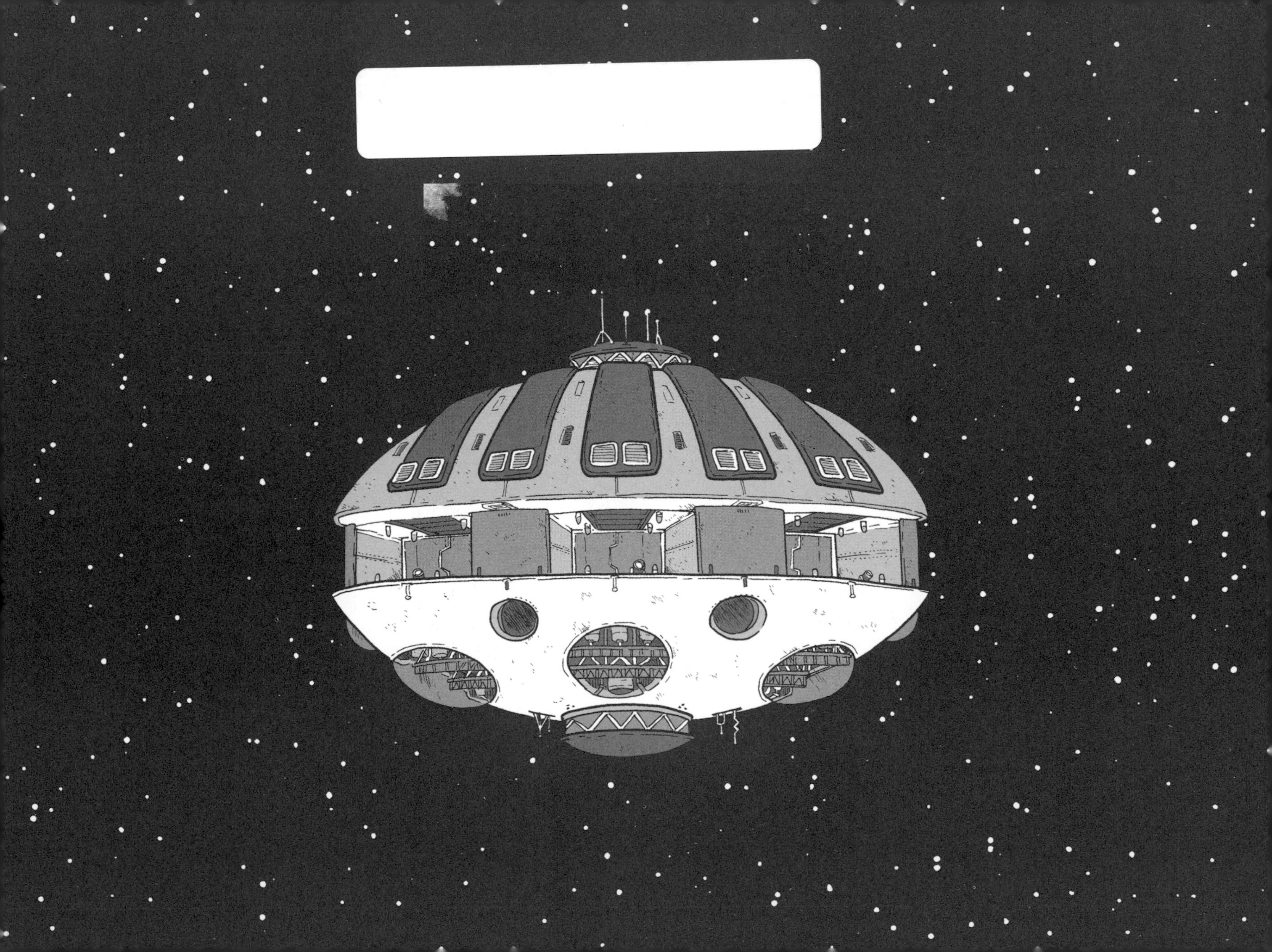

LEO GEO AND THE COSMIC CRISIS by jon chad
MultiCOM System 2.174
LOGIN:\>_MData

C:\>dir
dir:>fizzmont_institute_of_rad_science

COPYRIGHT © 2013 BY JON CHAD
PUBLISHED BY ROARING BROOK PRESS
ROARING BROOK PRESS IS A DIVISION OF HOLTZBRINCK
PUBLISHING HOLDINGS LIMITED PARTNERSHIP
175 FIFTH AVENUE, NEW YORK, NEW YORK 10010
MACKIDS.COM
ALL RIGHTS RESERVED

LIBRARY OF CONGRESS CATALOGING-IN-PUBLICATION DATA

CHAD, JON, AUTHOR, ILLUSTRATOR.
   LEO GEO AND THE COSMIC CRISIS / JON CHAD.—FIRST EDITION.
      PAGES CM
   SUMMARY: ARMED WITH HIS KNOWLEDGE OF SCIENCE, LEO GEO BECOMES AN ASTRONAUT
AND HEADS INTO SPACE, WHERE HE ENCOUNTERS PIRATES AND TRIES TO STOP A COMET
THAT IS HEADED TOWARD HIS BROTHER'S SCIENCE LABORATORY ON EARTH.
   ISBN 978-1-59643-822-4 (HARDCOVER)
1. GRAPHIC NOVELS. [1. GRAPHIC NOVELS. 2. SPACE FLIGHT—FICTION.
3. ASTRONAUTS—FICTION. 4. ADVENTURE AND ADVENTURERS—FICTION.
5. MAGIC—FICTION.] I. TITLE.

PZ7.7.C414LFC 2013
741.5'973—DC23

2013001296

ROARING BROOK PRESS BOOKS MAY BE PURCHASED FOR BUSINESS OR
PROMOTIONAL USE. FOR INFORMATION ON BULK PURCHASES PLEASE
CONTACT MACMILLAN CORPORATE AND PREMIUM SALES DEPARTMENT AT
(800) 221-7945 X5442 OR BY EMAIL AT SPECIALMARKETS@MACMILLAN.COM.

FIRST EDITION 2013
BOOK DESIGN BY JON CHAD
PRINTED IN CHINA BY TOPPAN LEEFUNG PRINTING LTD.,
DONGGUAN CITY, GUANGDONG PROVINCE

10 9 8 7 6 5 4 3 2 1

dir:>thanks

SPECIAL THANKS TO ROBYN C, COLLEEN F, SOPHIE G, BETH H, KATHERINE R, DENIS ST J, JEREMY S, SASHA S, LAURA T, AND ALL MY DRAWING BUDDIES. THANKS TO DEIRDRE L, ANDREW A, AND ANNE D FOR THE GUIDANCE. THANKS TO MY FAMILY AND FRIENDS FOR ALL THEIR SUPPORT. AN EXTRA SPECIAL THANKS TO ALEC L, LAUREL L, AND APRIL M FOR HELPING ME GET THROUGH SUMMER '12 UNSCATHED!

dir:>collophon

THIS BOOK WAS DRAWN WITH PIGMA MICRO MARKERS (SIZES 05, 01, AND 005), SPEEDBALL SUPERBLACK INDIA INK, AND MANY HUNT 102 CROW QUILLS ON 400 SERIES STRATHMORE SMOOTH BRISTOL BOARD.

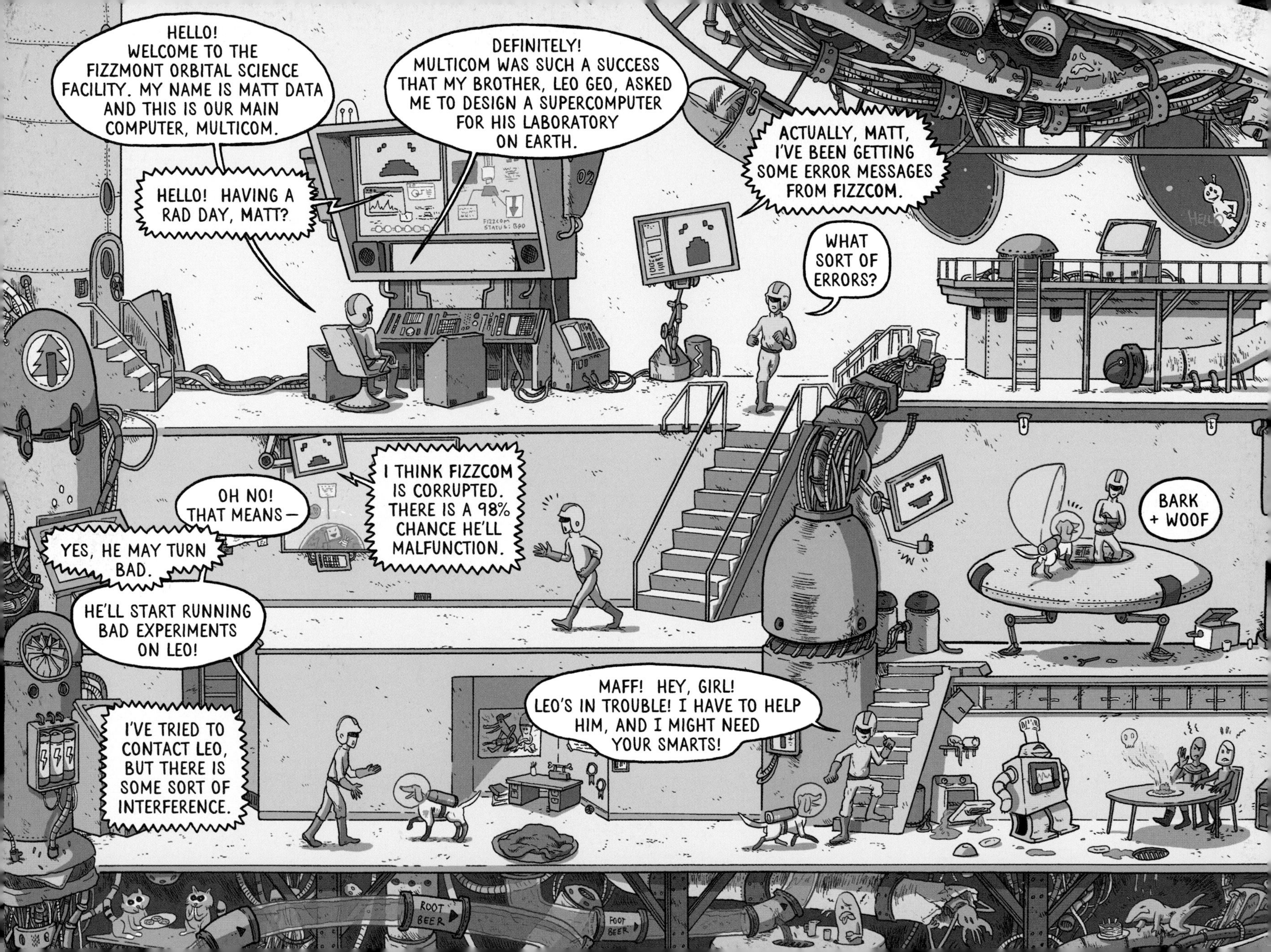
HELLO! WELCOME TO THE FIZZMONT ORBITAL SCIENCE FACILITY. MY NAME IS MATT DATA AND THIS IS OUR MAIN COMPUTER, MULTICOM.
HELLO! HAVING A RAD DAY, MATT?
DEFINITELY! MULTICOM WAS SUCH A SUCCESS THAT MY BROTHER, LEO GEO, ASKED ME TO DESIGN A SUPERCOMPUTER FOR HIS LABORATORY ON EARTH.
ACTUALLY, MATT, I'VE BEEN GETTING SOME ERROR MESSAGES FROM FIZZCOM.
WHAT SORT OF ERRORS?
I THINK FIZZCOM IS CORRUPTED. THERE IS A 98% CHANCE HE'LL MALFUNCTION.
OH NO! THAT MEANS—
YES, HE MAY TURN BAD.
HE'LL START RUNNING BAD EXPERIMENTS ON LEO!
I'VE TRIED TO CONTACT LEO, BUT THERE IS SOME SORT OF INTERFERENCE.
MAFF! HEY, GIRL! LEO'S IN TROUBLE! I HAVE TO HELP HIM, AND I MIGHT NEED YOUR SMARTS!
BARK + WOOF
ROOT BEER
ROOT BEER

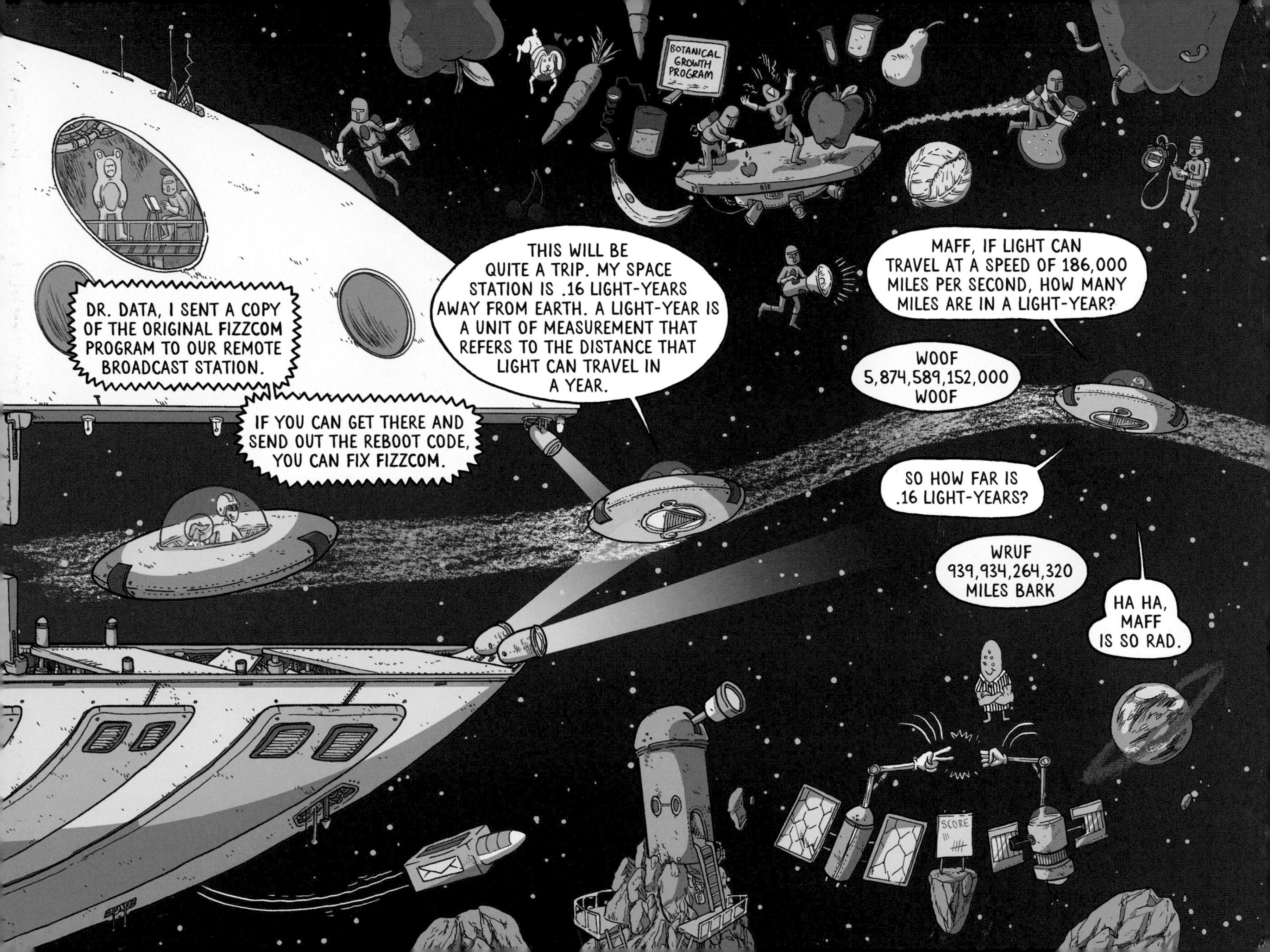
DR. DATA, I SENT A COPY OF THE ORIGINAL FIZZCOM PROGRAM TO OUR REMOTE BROADCAST STATION.
IF YOU CAN GET THERE AND SEND OUT THE REBOOT CODE, YOU CAN FIX FIZZCOM.
THIS WILL BE QUITE A TRIP. MY SPACE STATION IS .16 LIGHT-YEARS AWAY FROM EARTH. A LIGHT-YEAR IS A UNIT OF MEASUREMENT THAT REFERS TO THE DISTANCE THAT LIGHT CAN TRAVEL IN A YEAR.
MAFF, IF LIGHT CAN TRAVEL AT A SPEED OF 186,000 MILES PER SECOND, HOW MANY MILES ARE IN A LIGHT-YEAR?
WOOF 5,874,589,152,000 WOOF
SO HOW FAR IS .16 LIGHT-YEARS?
WRUF 939,934,264,320 MILES BARK
HA HA, MAFF IS SO RAD.
BOTANICAL GROWTH PROGRAM
SCORE

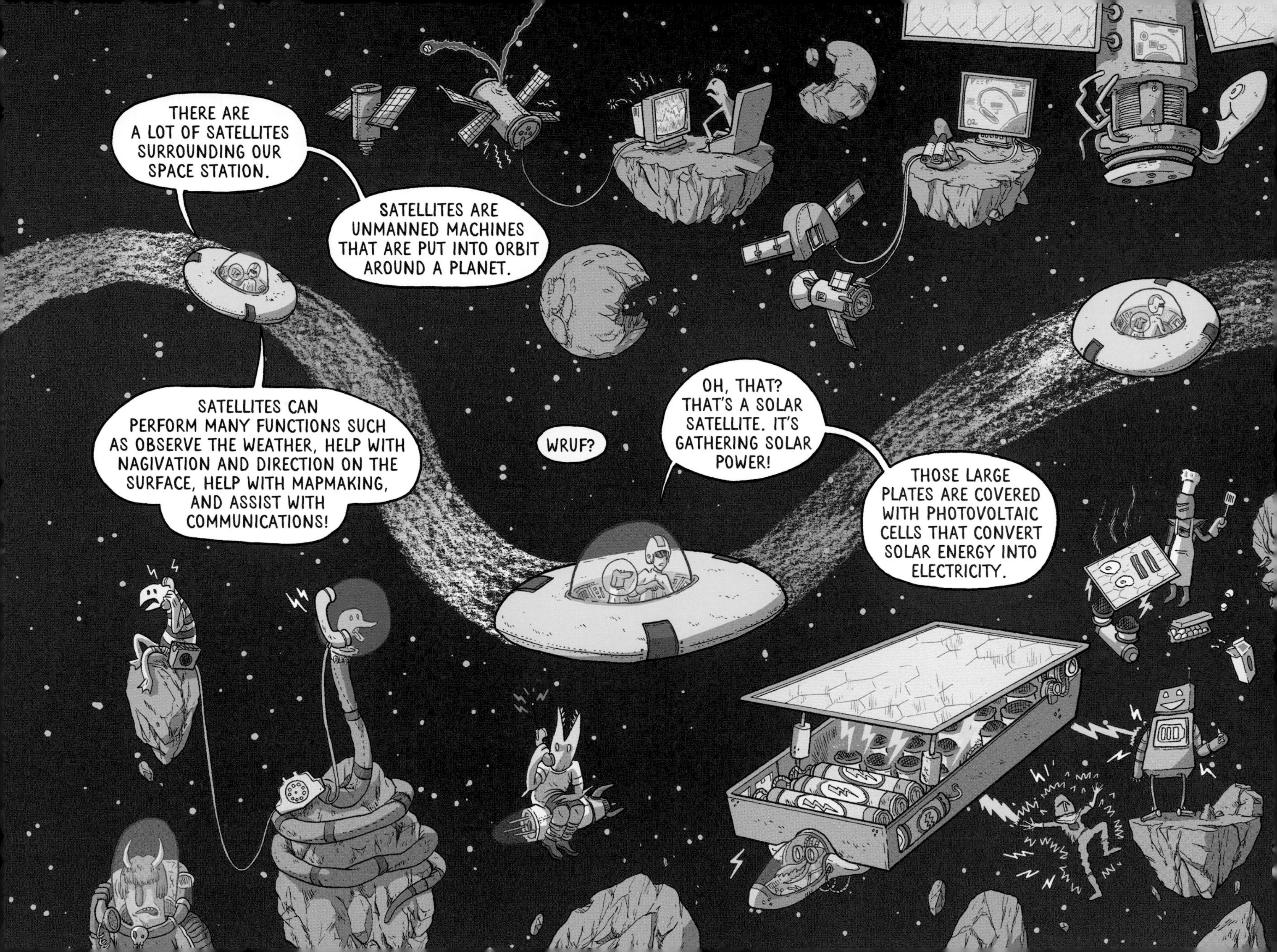
THERE ARE A LOT OF SATELLITES SURROUNDING OUR SPACE STATION.
SATELLITES ARE UNMANNED MACHINES THAT ARE PUT INTO ORBIT AROUND A PLANET.
SATELLITES CAN PERFORM MANY FUNCTIONS SUCH AS OBSERVE THE WEATHER, HELP WITH NAGIVATION AND DIRECTION ON THE SURFACE, HELP WITH MAPMAKING, AND ASSIST WITH COMMUNICATIONS!
WRUF?
OH, THAT? THAT'S A SOLAR SATELLITE. IT'S GATHERING SOLAR POWER!
THOSE LARGE PLATES ARE COVERED WITH PHOTOVOLTAIC CELLS THAT CONVERT SOLAR ENERGY INTO ELECTRICITY.

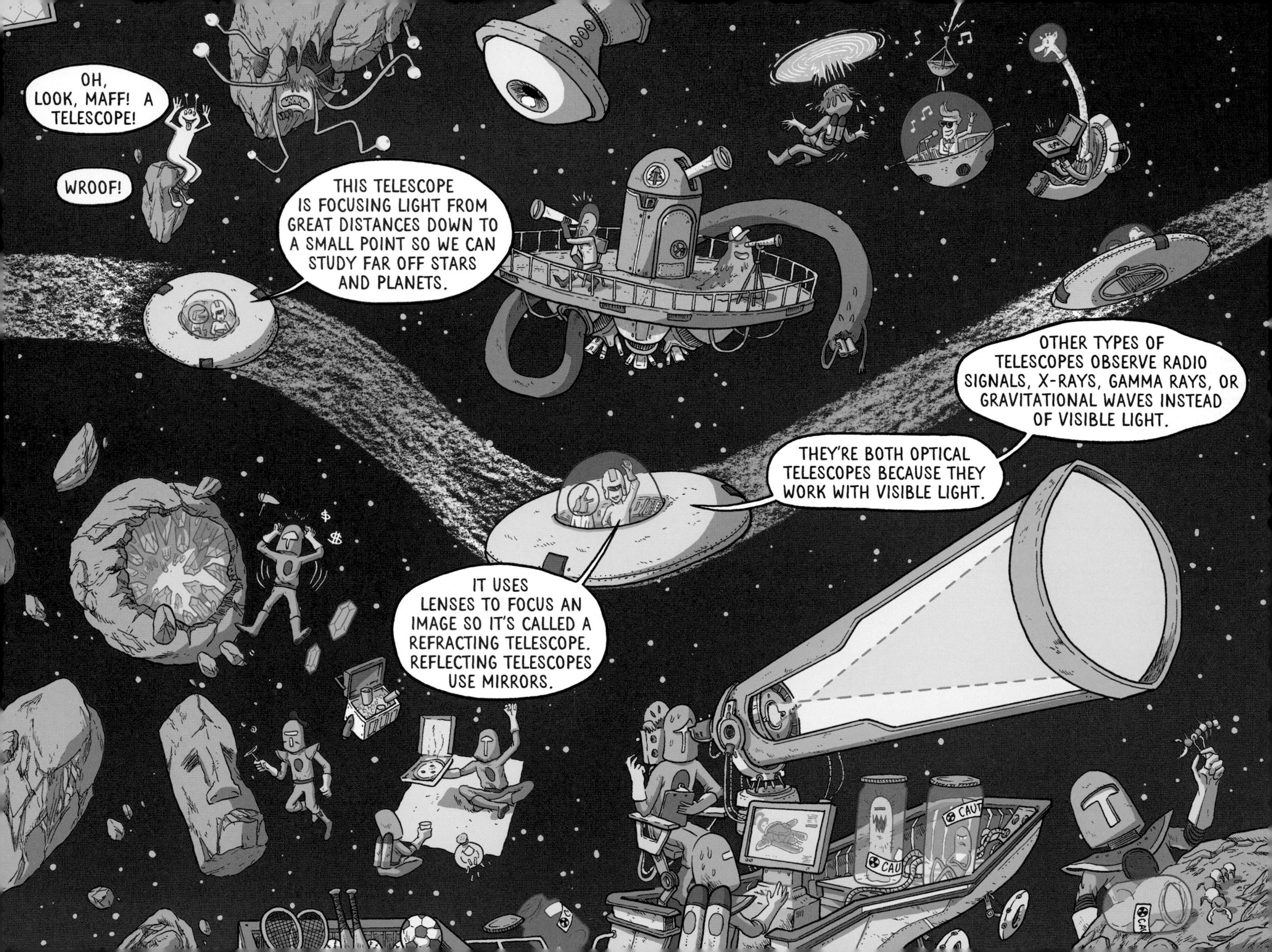
OH, LOOK, MAFF! A TELESCOPE!
WROOF!
THIS TELESCOPE IS FOCUSING LIGHT FROM GREAT DISTANCES DOWN TO A SMALL POINT SO WE CAN STUDY FAR OFF STARS AND PLANETS.
OTHER TYPES OF TELESCOPES OBSERVE RADIO SIGNALS, X-RAYS, GAMMA RAYS, OR GRAVITATIONAL WAVES INSTEAD OF VISIBLE LIGHT.
THEY'RE BOTH OPTICAL TELESCOPES BECAUSE THEY WORK WITH VISIBLE LIGHT.
IT USES LENSES TO FOCUS AN IMAGE SO IT'S CALLED A REFRACTING TELESCOPE. REFLECTING TELESCOPES USE MIRRORS.

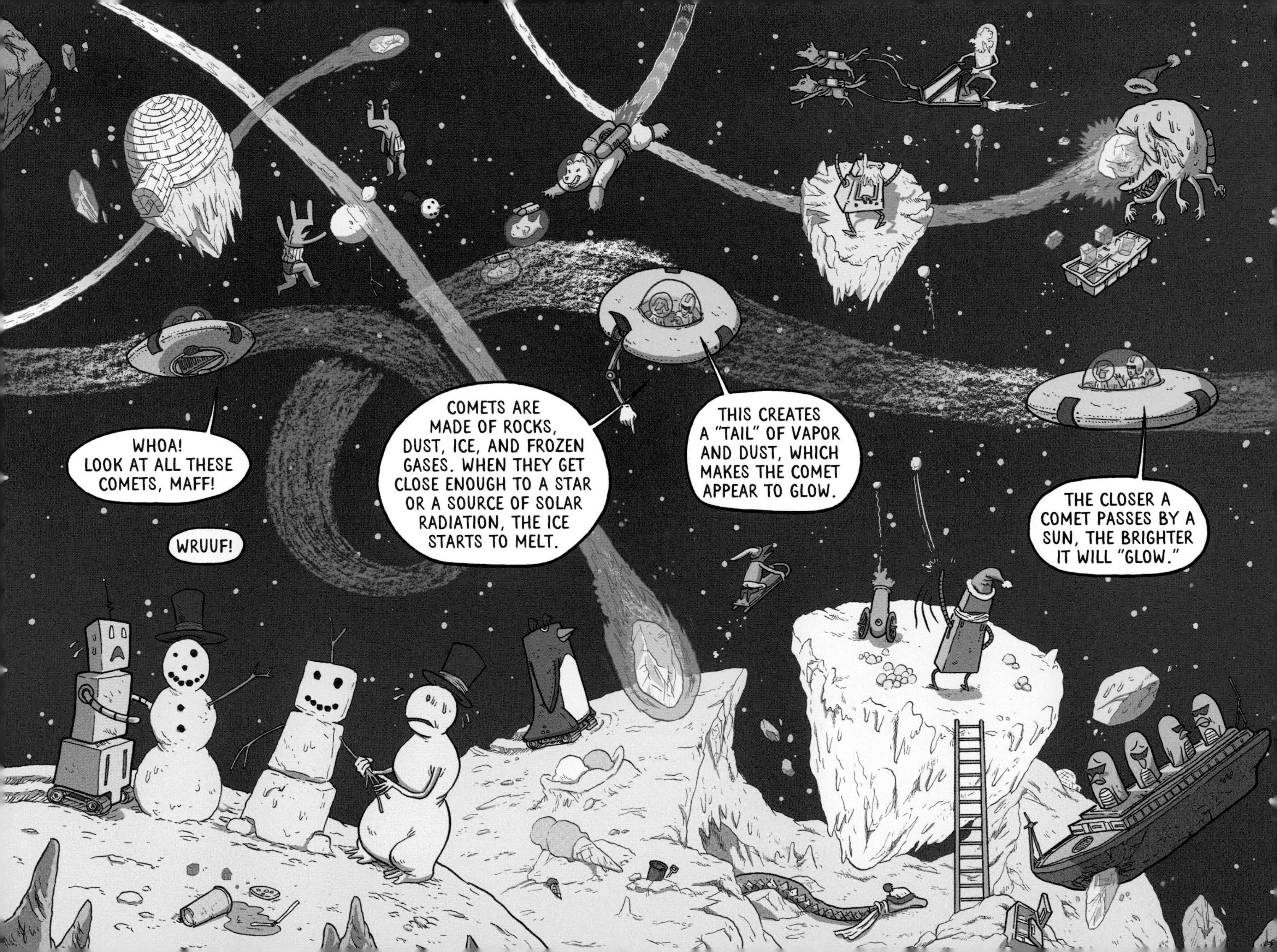
WHOA! LOOK AT ALL THESE COMETS, MAFF!
WRUUF!
COMETS ARE MADE OF ROCKS, DUST, ICE, AND FROZEN GASES. WHEN THEY GET CLOSE ENOUGH TO A STAR OR A SOURCE OF SOLAR RADIATION, THE ICE STARTS TO MELT.
THIS CREATES A "TAIL" OF VAPOR AND DUST, WHICH MAKES THE COMET APPEAR TO GLOW.
THE CLOSER A COMET PASSES BY A SUN, THE BRIGHTER IT WILL "GLOW."

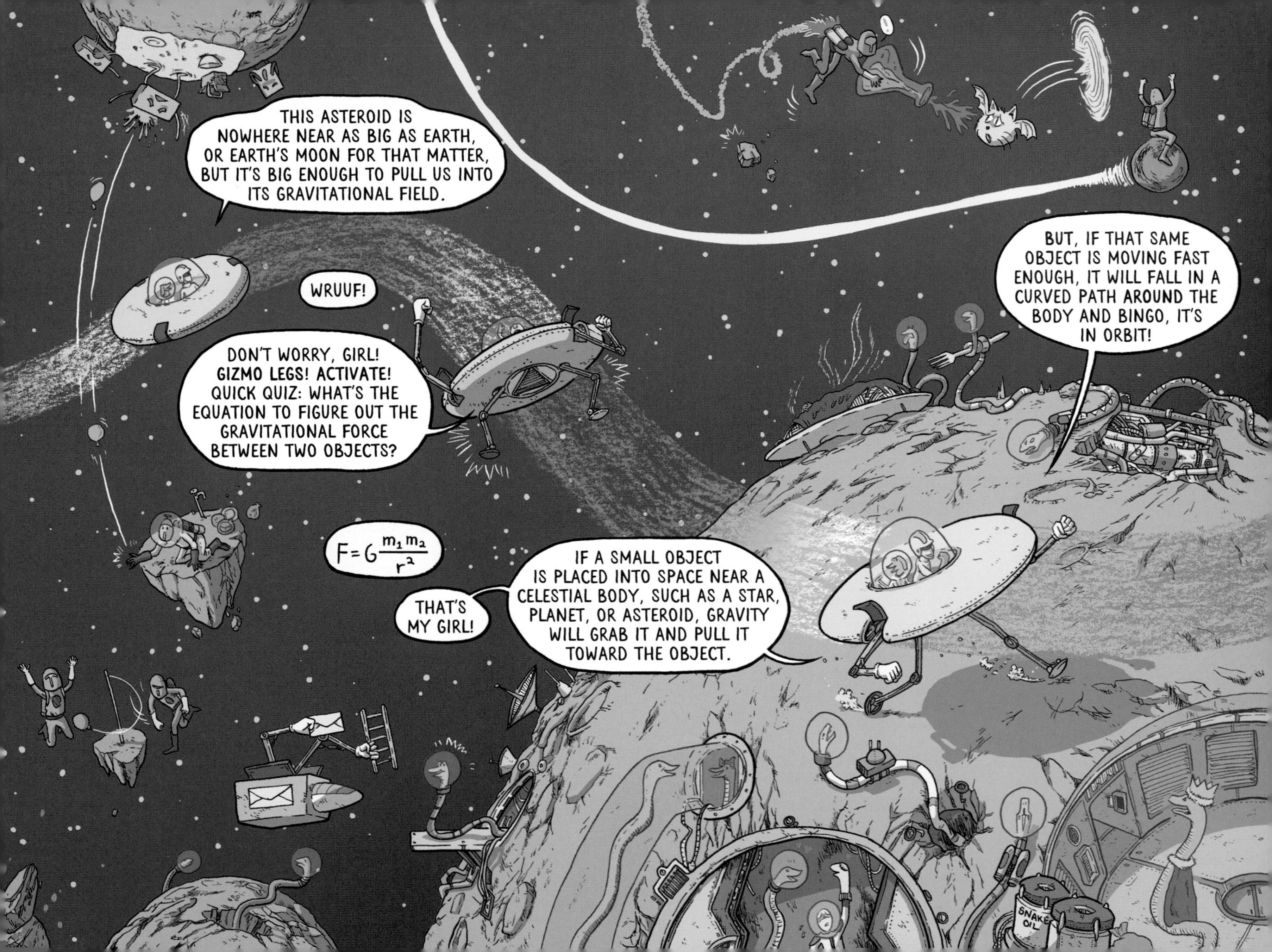
THIS ASTEROID IS NOWHERE NEAR AS BIG AS EARTH, OR EARTH'S MOON FOR THAT MATTER, BUT IT'S BIG ENOUGH TO PULL US INTO ITS GRAVITATIONAL FIELD.
WRUUF!
DON'T WORRY, GIRL! GIZMO LEGS! ACTIVATE! QUICK QUIZ: WHAT'S THE EQUATION TO FIGURE OUT THE GRAVITATIONAL FORCE BETWEEN TWO OBJECTS?
$F = G\frac{m_1 m_2}{r^2}$
THAT'S MY GIRL!
IF A SMALL OBJECT IS PLACED INTO SPACE NEAR A CELESTIAL BODY, SUCH AS A STAR, PLANET, OR ASTEROID, GRAVITY WILL GRAB IT AND PULL IT TOWARD THE OBJECT.
BUT, IF THAT SAME OBJECT IS MOVING FAST ENOUGH, IT WILL FALL IN A CURVED PATH AROUND THE BODY AND BINGO, IT'S IN ORBIT!
SNAKE OIL

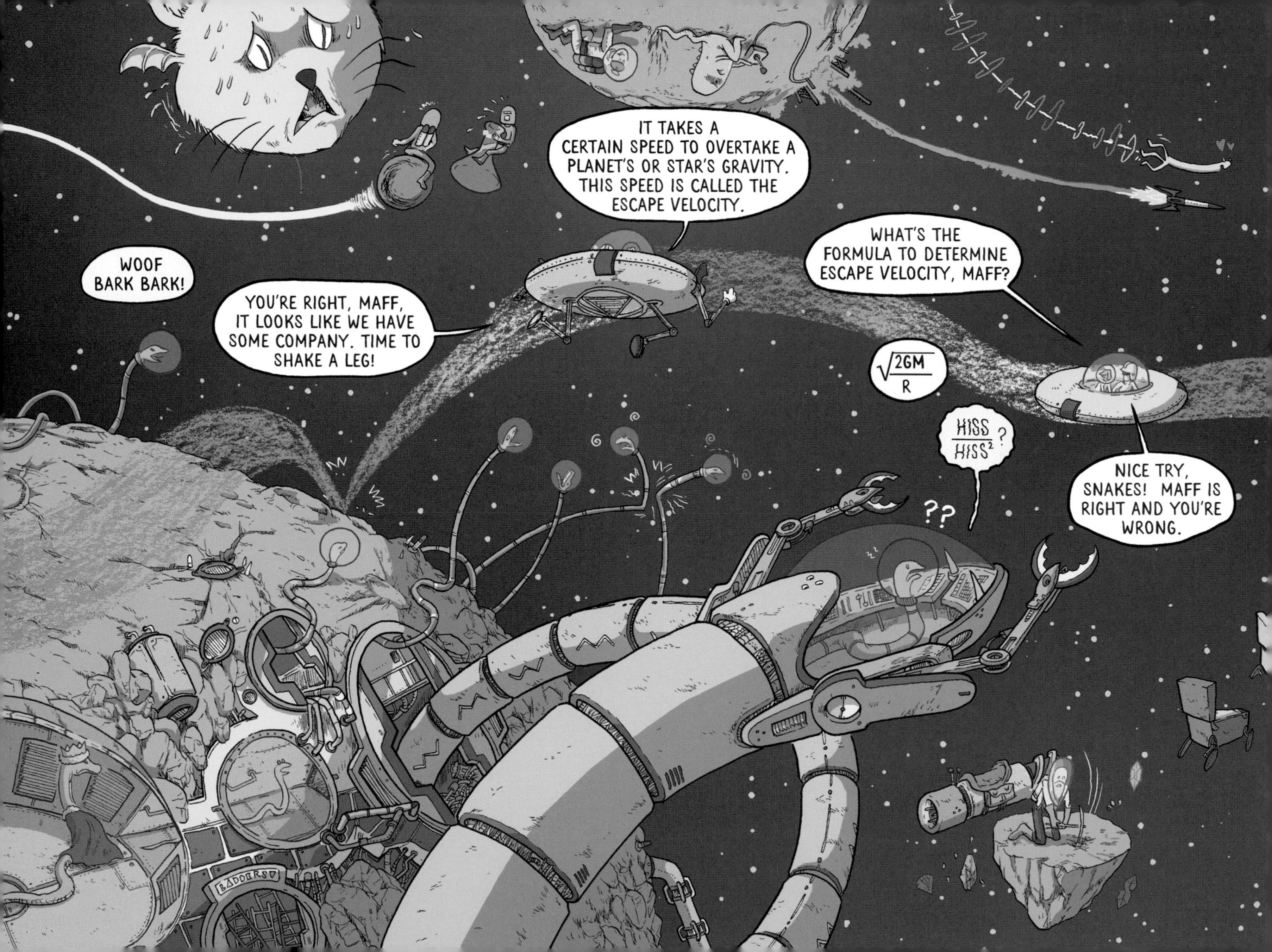
IT TAKES A CERTAIN SPEED TO OVERTAKE A PLANET'S OR STAR'S GRAVITY. THIS SPEED IS CALLED THE ESCAPE VELOCITY.
WHAT'S THE FORMULA TO DETERMINE ESCAPE VELOCITY, MAFF?
WOOF BARK BARK!
YOU'RE RIGHT, MAFF, IT LOOKS LIKE WE HAVE SOME COMPANY. TIME TO SHAKE A LEG!
$\sqrt{\frac{2GM}{R}}$
$\frac{HISS}{HISS^2}$?
NICE TRY, SNAKES! MAFF IS RIGHT AND YOU'RE WRONG.
??
BADDERS

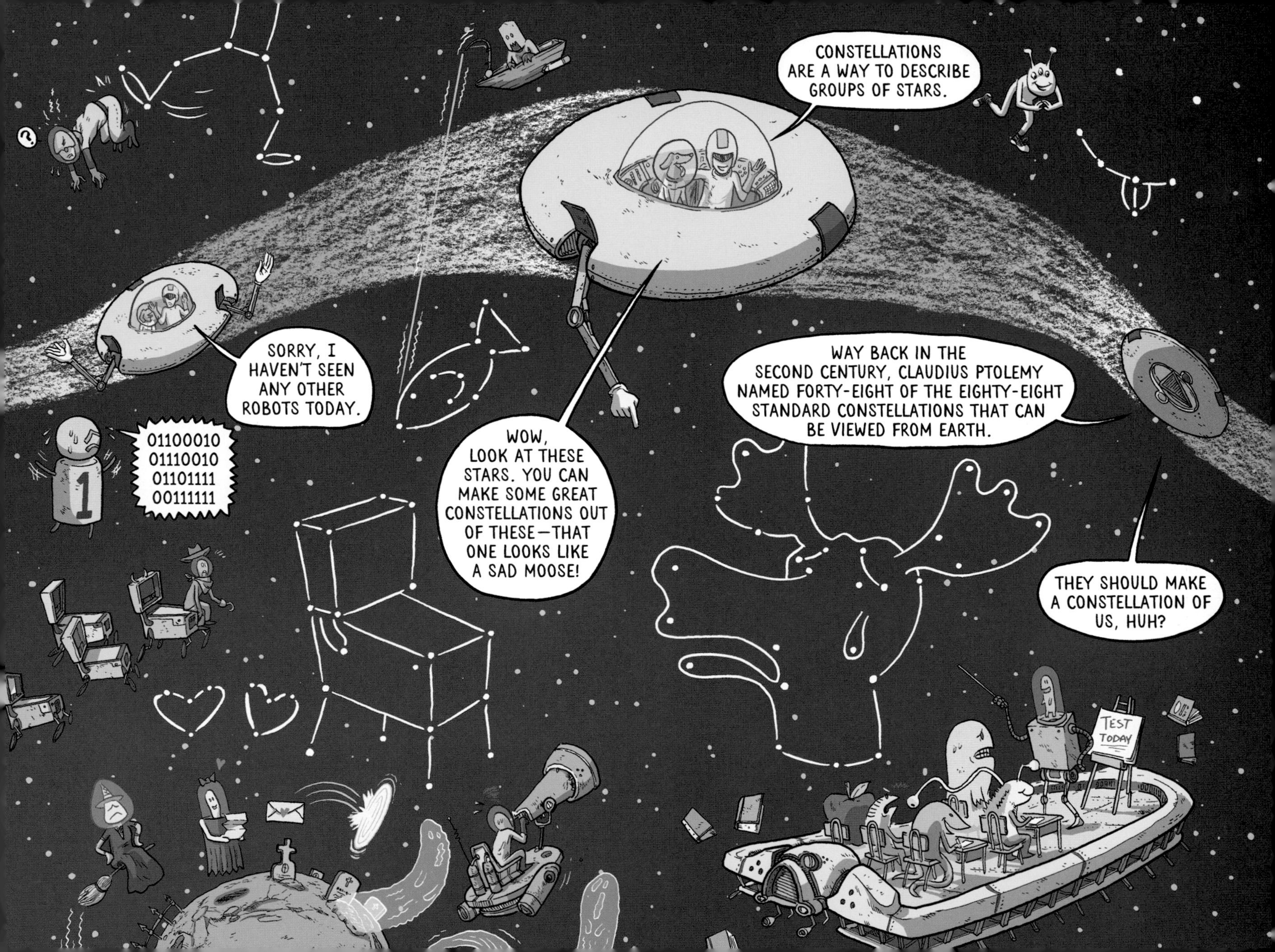
CONSTELLATIONS ARE A WAY TO DESCRIBE GROUPS OF STARS.
WOW, LOOK AT THESE STARS. YOU CAN MAKE SOME GREAT CONSTELLATIONS OUT OF THESE—THAT ONE LOOKS LIKE A SAD MOOSE!
WAY BACK IN THE SECOND CENTURY, CLAUDIUS PTOLEMY NAMED FORTY-EIGHT OF THE EIGHTY-EIGHT STANDARD CONSTELLATIONS THAT CAN BE VIEWED FROM EARTH.
THEY SHOULD MAKE A CONSTELLATION OF US, HUH?
SORRY, I HAVEN'T SEEN ANY OTHER ROBOTS TODAY.
01100010 01110010 01101111 00111111
1
TEST TODAY

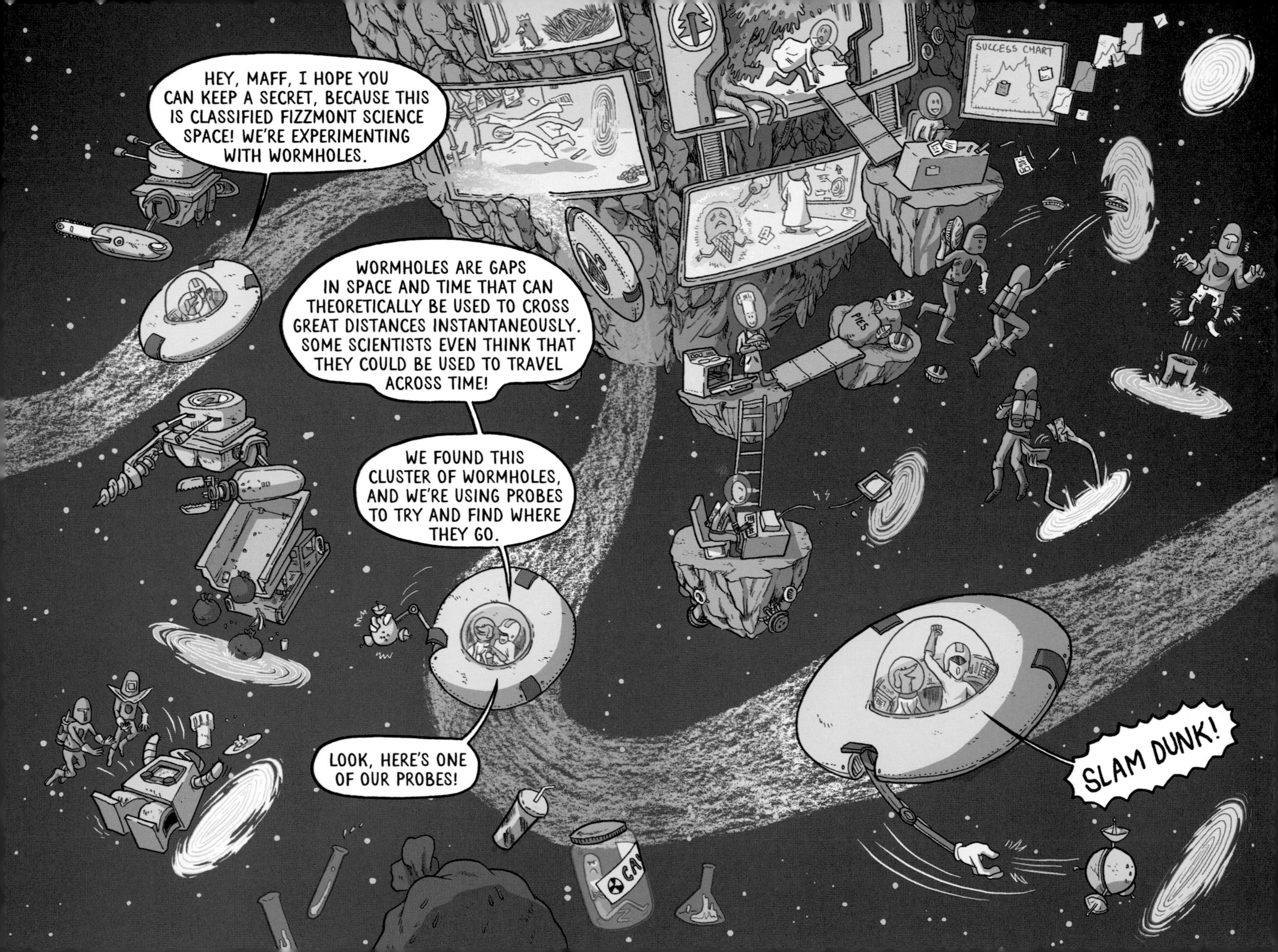
HEY, MAFF, I HOPE YOU CAN KEEP A SECRET, BECAUSE THIS IS CLASSIFIED FIZZMONT SCIENCE SPACE! WE'RE EXPERIMENTING WITH WORMHOLES.
WORMHOLES ARE GAPS IN SPACE AND TIME THAT CAN THEORETICALLY BE USED TO CROSS GREAT DISTANCES INSTANTANEOUSLY. SOME SCIENTISTS EVEN THINK THAT THEY COULD BE USED TO TRAVEL ACROSS TIME!
WE FOUND THIS CLUSTER OF WORMHOLES, AND WE'RE USING PROBES TO TRY AND FIND WHERE THEY GO.
LOOK, HERE'S ONE OF OUR PROBES!
SLAM DUNK!
SUCCESS CHART
PIES

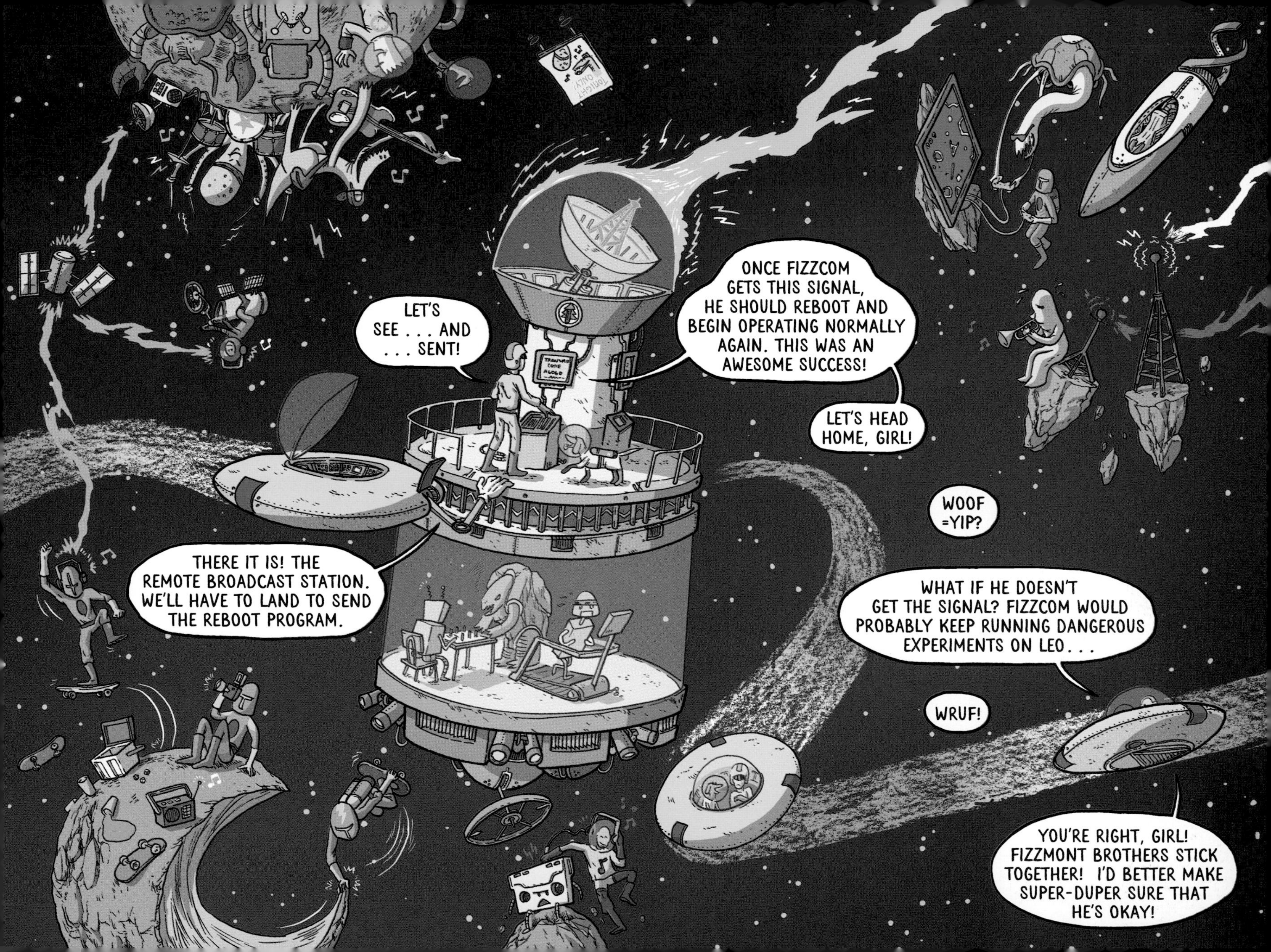

TONIGHT ONLY!
LET'S SEE . . . AND . . . SENT!
ONCE FIZZCOM GETS THIS SIGNAL, HE SHOULD REBOOT AND BEGIN OPERATING NORMALLY AGAIN. THIS WAS AN AWESOME SUCCESS!
LET'S HEAD HOME, GIRL!
THERE IT IS! THE REMOTE BROADCAST STATION. WE'LL HAVE TO LAND TO SEND THE REBOOT PROGRAM.
WOOF =YIP?
WHAT IF HE DOESN'T GET THE SIGNAL? FIZZCOM WOULD PROBABLY KEEP RUNNING DANGEROUS EXPERIMENTS ON LEO . . .
WRUF!
YOU'RE RIGHT, GIRL! FIZZMONT BROTHERS STICK TOGETHER! I'D BETTER MAKE SUPER-DUPER SURE THAT HE'S OKAY!

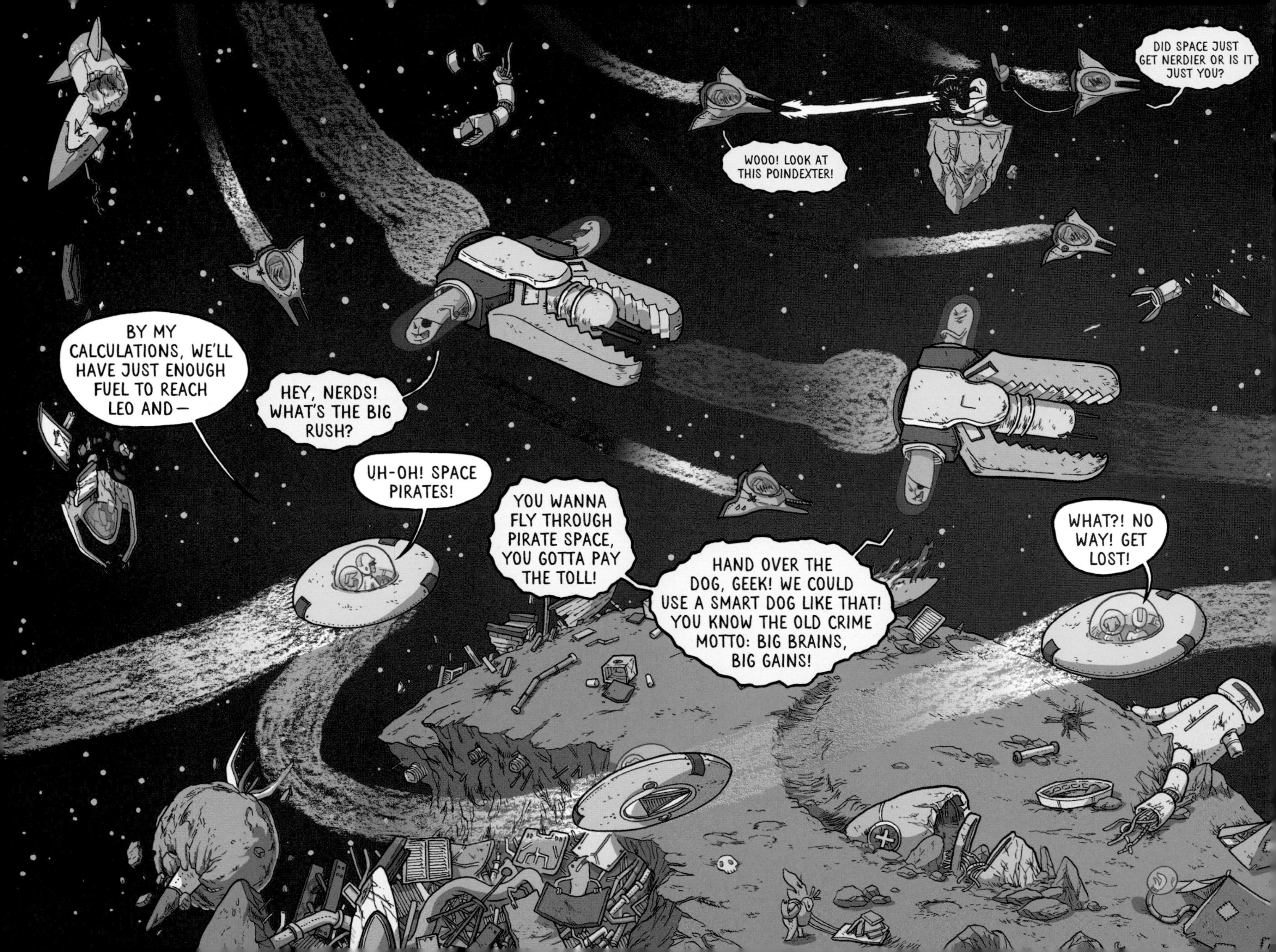
BY MY CALCULATIONS, WE'LL HAVE JUST ENOUGH FUEL TO REACH LEO AND—
HEY, NERDS! WHAT'S THE BIG RUSH?
UH-OH! SPACE PIRATES!
YOU WANNA FLY THROUGH PIRATE SPACE, YOU GOTTA PAY THE TOLL!
HAND OVER THE DOG, GEEK! WE COULD USE A SMART DOG LIKE THAT! YOU KNOW THE OLD CRIME MOTTO: BIG BRAINS, BIG GAINS!
WHAT?! NO WAY! GET LOST!
WOOO! LOOK AT THIS POINDEXTER!
DID SPACE JUST GET NERDIER OR IS IT JUST YOU?

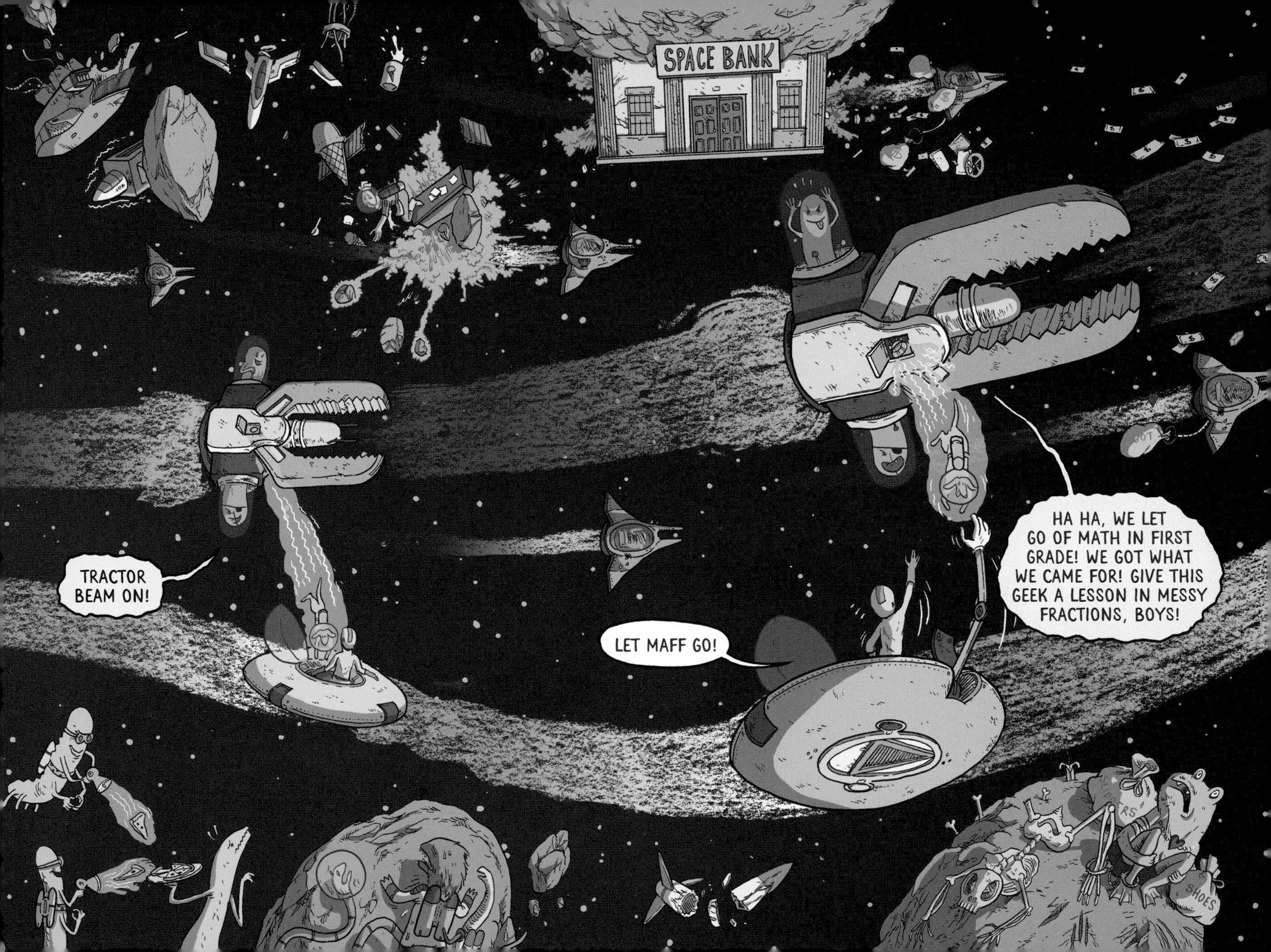
SPACE BANK
TRACTOR BEAM ON!
LET MAFF GO!
HA HA, WE LET GO OF MATH IN FIRST GRADE! WE GOT WHAT WE CAME FOR! GIVE THIS GEEK A LESSON IN MESSY FRACTIONS, BOYS!
SHOES

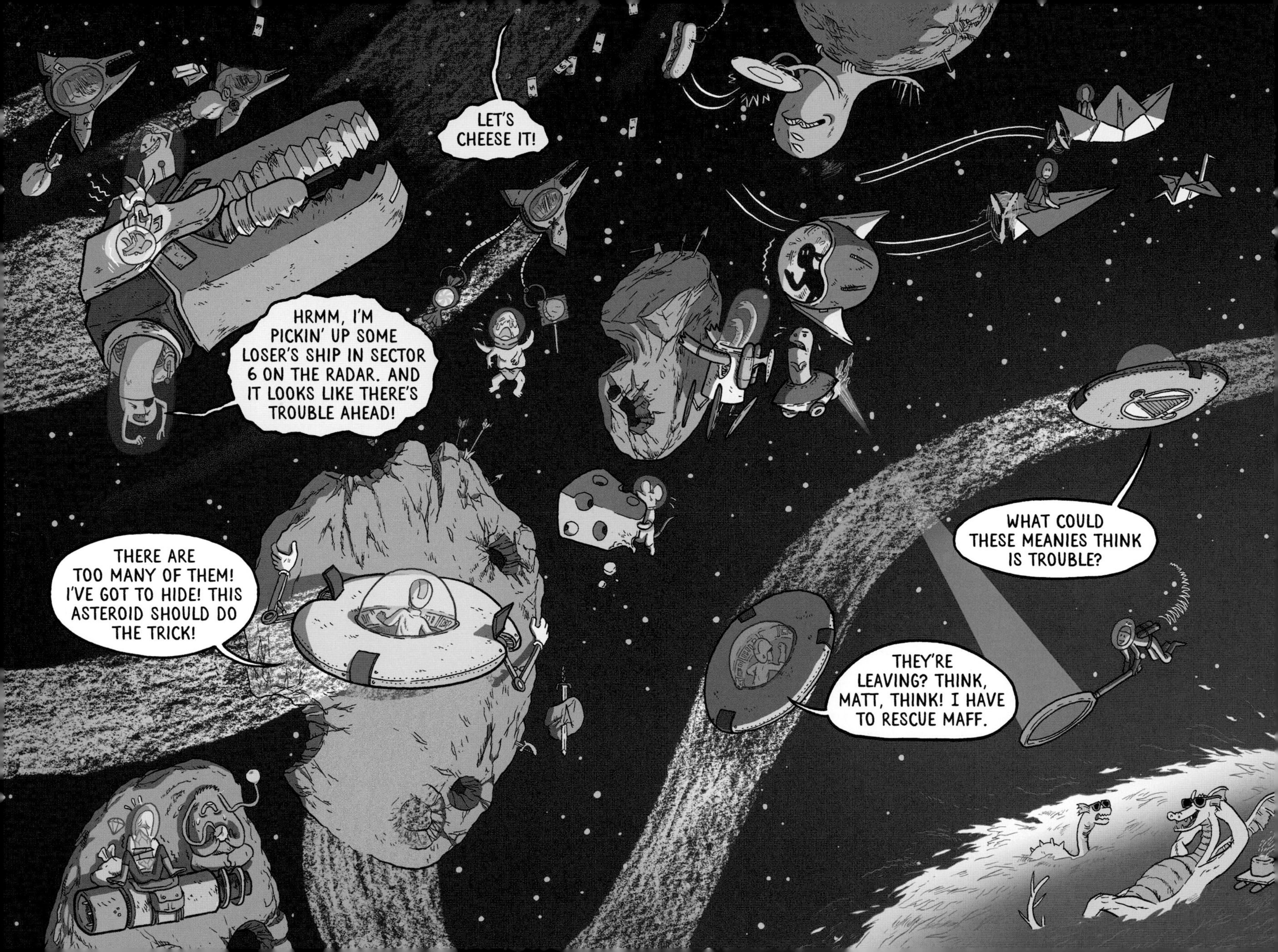
LET'S CHEESE IT!
HRMM, I'M PICKIN' UP SOME LOSER'S SHIP IN SECTOR 6 ON THE RADAR. AND IT LOOKS LIKE THERE'S TROUBLE AHEAD!
THERE ARE TOO MANY OF THEM! I'VE GOT TO HIDE! THIS ASTEROID SHOULD DO THE TRICK!
WHAT COULD THESE MEANIES THINK IS TROUBLE?
THEY'RE LEAVING? THINK, MATT, THINK! I HAVE TO RESCUE MAFF.

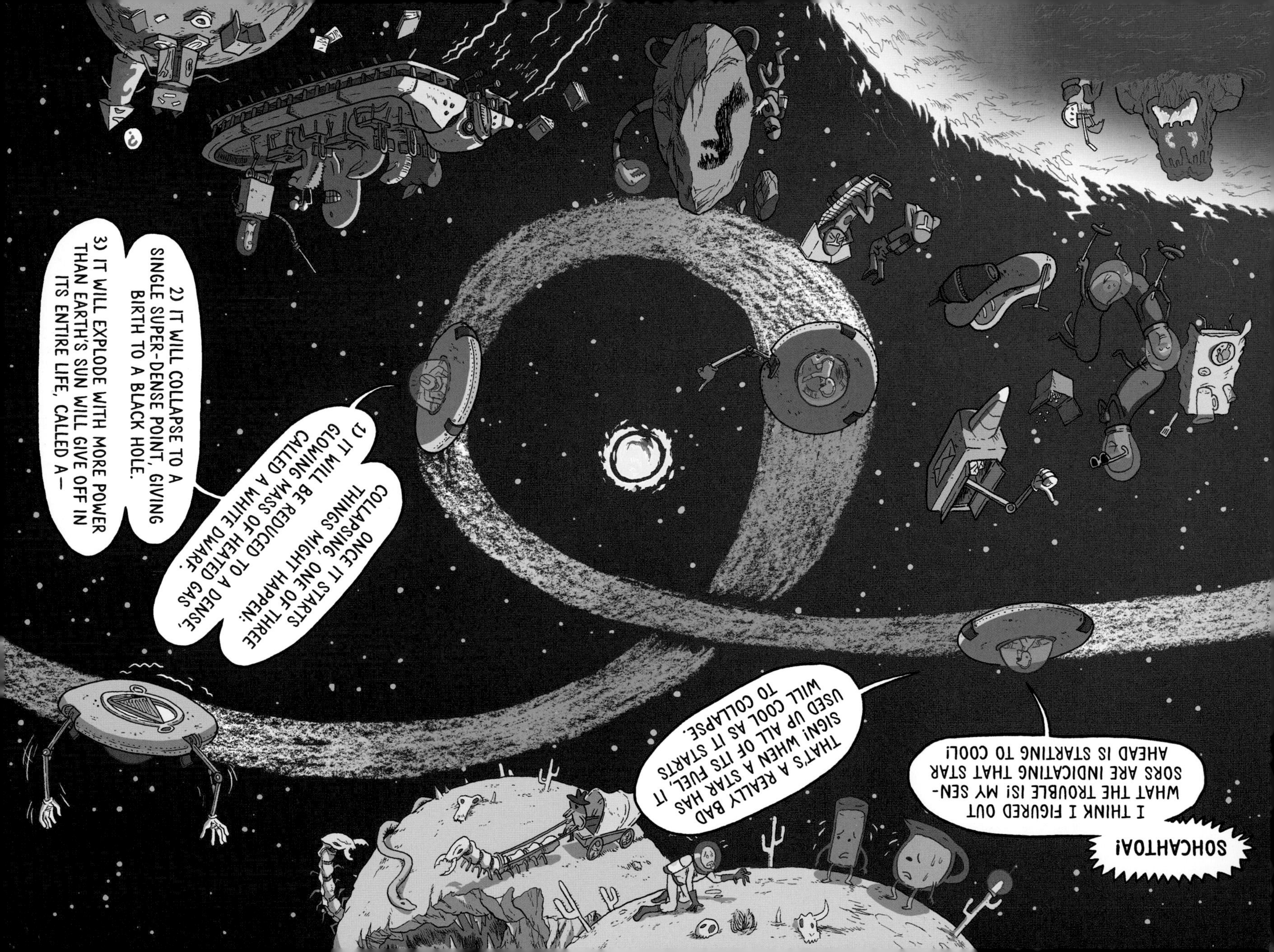
SOHCAHTOA!
I THINK I FIGURED OUT WHAT THE TROUBLE IS! MY SEN-SORS ARE INDICATING THAT STAR AHEAD IS STARTING TO COOL!
THAT'S A REALLY BAD SIGN! WHEN A STAR HAS USED UP ALL OF ITS FUEL, IT WILL COOL AS IT STARTS TO COLLAPSE.
ONCE IT STARTS COLLAPSING, ONE OF THREE THINGS MIGHT HAPPEN: 1) IT WILL BE REDUCED TO A DENSE, GLOWING MASS OF HEATED GAS, CALLED A WHITE DWARF.
2) IT WILL COLLAPSE TO A SINGLE SUPER-DENSE POINT, GIVING BIRTH TO A BLACK HOLE.
3) IT WILL EXPLODE WITH MORE POWER THAN EARTH'S SUN WILL GIVE OFF IN ITS ENTIRE LIFE, CALLED A—

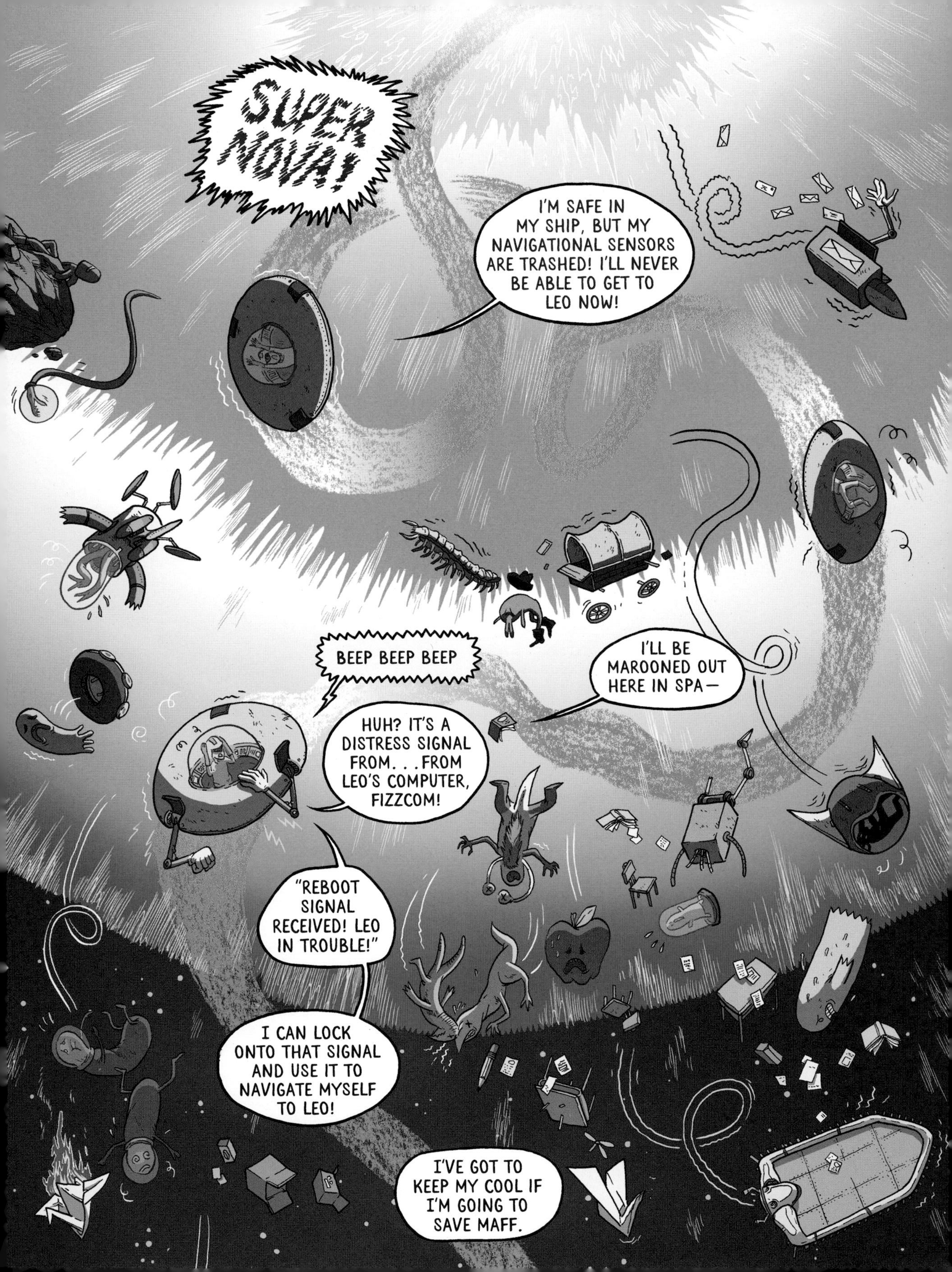
SUPER NOVA!
I'M SAFE IN MY SHIP, BUT MY NAVIGATIONAL SENSORS ARE TRASHED! I'LL NEVER BE ABLE TO GET TO LEO NOW!
I'LL BE MAROONED OUT HERE IN SPA—
BEEP BEEP BEEP
HUH? IT'S A DISTRESS SIGNAL FROM. . .FROM LEO'S COMPUTER, FIZZCOM!
"REBOOT SIGNAL RECEIVED! LEO IN TROUBLE!"
I CAN LOCK ONTO THAT SIGNAL AND USE IT TO NAVIGATE MYSELF TO LEO!
I'VE GOT TO KEEP MY COOL IF I'M GOING TO SAVE MAFF.

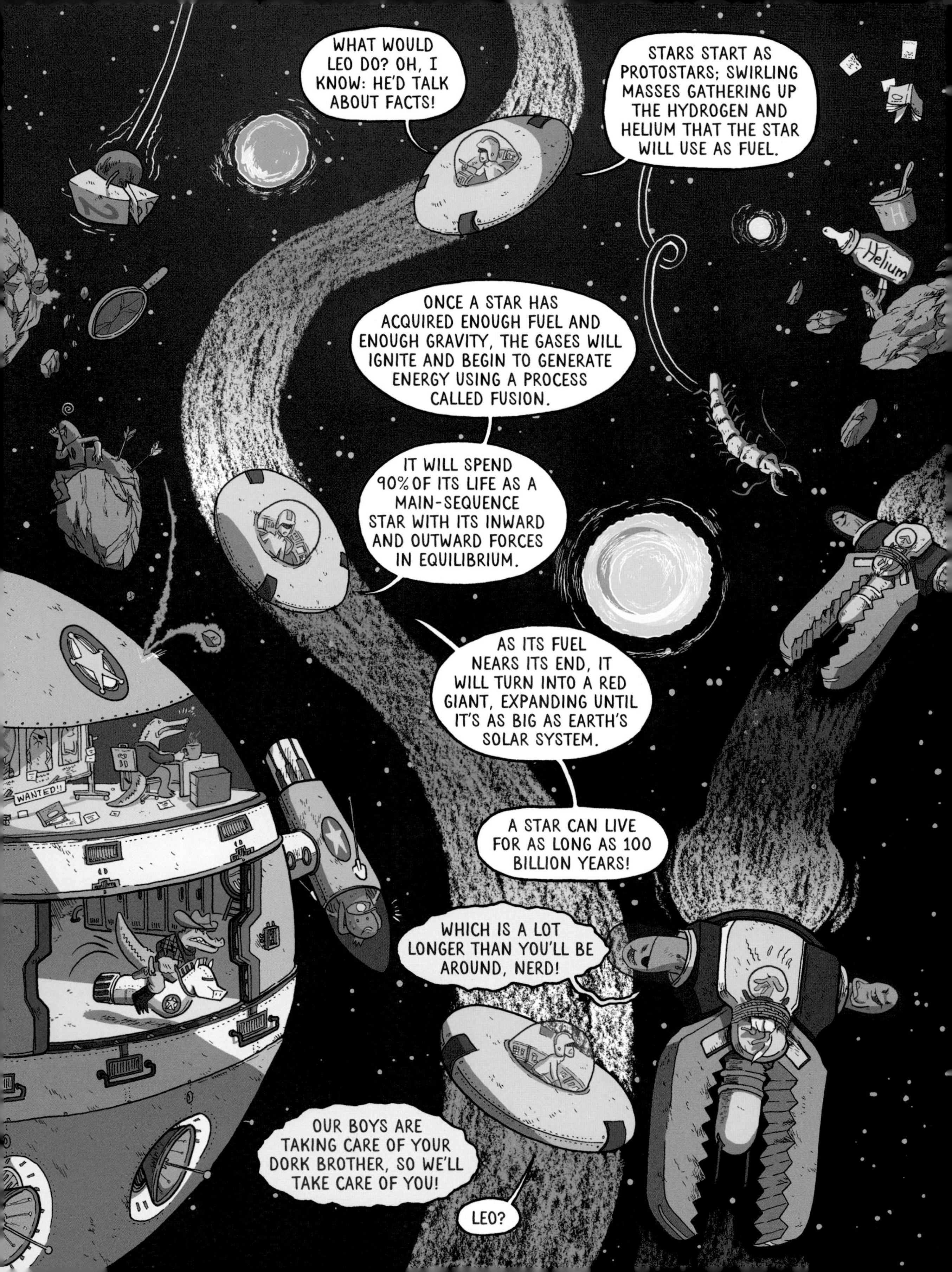

WHAT WOULD LEO DO? OH, I KNOW: HE'D TALK ABOUT FACTS!
STARS START AS PROTOSTARS; SWIRLING MASSES GATHERING UP THE HYDROGEN AND HELIUM THAT THE STAR WILL USE AS FUEL.
Helium
H
ONCE A STAR HAS ACQUIRED ENOUGH FUEL AND ENOUGH GRAVITY, THE GASES WILL IGNITE AND BEGIN TO GENERATE ENERGY USING A PROCESS CALLED FUSION.
IT WILL SPEND 90% OF ITS LIFE AS A MAIN-SEQUENCE STAR WITH ITS INWARD AND OUTWARD FORCES IN EQUILIBRIUM.
AS ITS FUEL NEARS ITS END, IT WILL TURN INTO A RED GIANT, EXPANDING UNTIL IT'S AS BIG AS EARTH'S SOLAR SYSTEM.
A STAR CAN LIVE FOR AS LONG AS 100 BILLION YEARS!
WANTED!!
WHICH IS A LOT LONGER THAN YOU'LL BE AROUND, NERD!
OUR BOYS ARE TAKING CARE OF YOUR DORK BROTHER, SO WE'LL TAKE CARE OF YOU!
LEO?

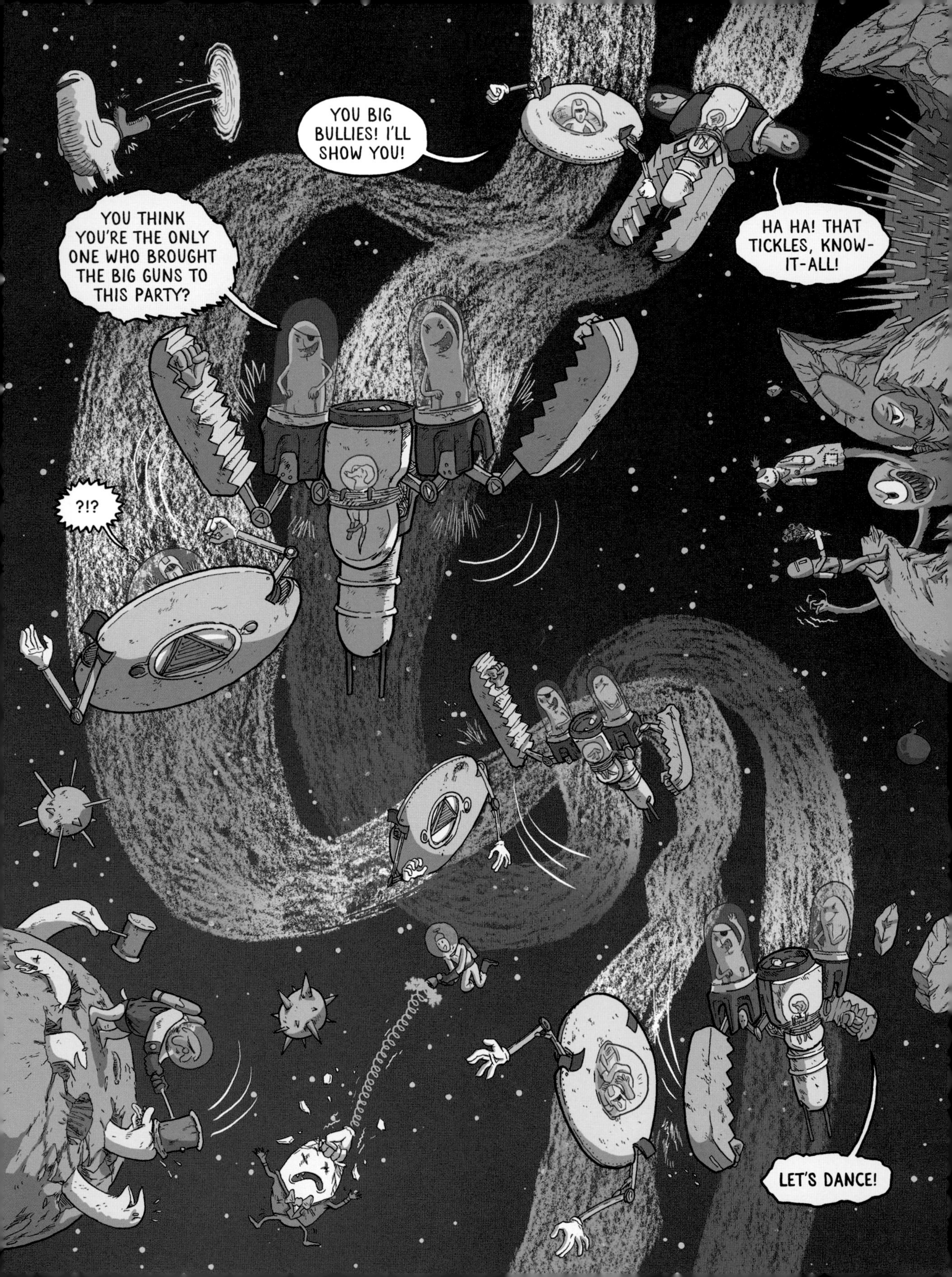
YOU BIG BULLIES! I'LL SHOW YOU!
YOU THINK YOU'RE THE ONLY ONE WHO BROUGHT THE BIG GUNS TO THIS PARTY?
HA HA! THAT TICKLES, KNOW-IT-ALL!
?!?
LET'S DANCE!